Listen to Your Heart

Listen to Your Heart

A Pride and Prejudice Variation

LEENIE BROWN

No part of this book may be reproduced in any form, except in the case of brief quotations embodied in critical articles or reviews, without written permission from its publisher and author.

This book is a work of fiction. All names, events, and places are a product of this author's imagination. If any name, event and/or place did exist, it is purely by coincidence that it appears in this book.

Listen to Your Heart © Leenie Brown. All Rights Reserved, except where otherwise noted.

Dedication

To my friend, Kathleen, who has always encouraged me to follow my heart and chase my daydreams

Thank you!

Contents

Chapter 1 1

Chapter 2 11

Chapter 3 23

Chapter 4 39

Chapter 5 55

Chapter 6 67

Chapter 7 79

Chapter 8 93

Chapter 9 105

Chapter 10 123

Chapter 11 135

Chapter 12 149

Chapter 13 163

Chapter 14 173

Chapter 15 185

Chapter 16 195

Chapter 17 207

Acknowledgements 219

About the Author 221
Connect with Leenie Brown 223
More from Leenie Brown 224

Chapter 1

"Did you read the papers I sent you?" Anne de Bourgh questioned her cousin Fitzwilliam Darcy as soon as he entered the sitting room.

"I did." He nodded to Mrs. Jenkins. She smiled and inclined her head in acceptance of his greeting before returning her focus to her stitching.

"And?" She looked at him expectantly, waiting for him to share his opinion of their content.

"You found them in your father's office?"

Anne nodded. "Between some books as if tucked away and out of sight intentionally."

"I had my solicitor look at them. They seem legitimate." He tipped his head to the side and gave her a questioning look. "They will change things for your mother. Are you sure you wish to take on that battle? Will your health tolerate it?"

"My health will never be robust, but I am not standing on the edge of the grave, Fitzwilliam." Anne laid aside her mending. "I intend to approach her today on one item."

"Today?" Darcy handed Anne a small glass of sherry and then picking up his own glass, settled into a comfortable chair near his cousin. "And what item is first on your list?"

Anne sipped her sherry and considered how she should approach the subject of their supposed engagement. "I have heard some troubling news. It seems my mother's imaginings regarding our future have travelled far and wide."

"She has never been one to keep that particular story to herself. I am surprised you had not realized the extent to which it is common knowledge. Makes it blasted hard to get to know any young ladies during the season — which, I suppose, is her intent in publishing the tale." His eyes narrowed, and his jaw clenched as he attempted to contain his frustration at his aunt's machinations.

"Yes, but at least you are free of these walls." Anne waved a hand around the room. "I have not even been given the opportunity to meet any eligible gentlemen, and I am nearly five and twenty! Firmly on the shelf having never left it! No longer. I will have it no longer."

Darcy's eyes grew wide in surprise.

"Today, my mother will know that her imaginings are just that — fanciful tales which hold no basis in reality. I am sorry, my dear cousin, but I do not now, nor have I ever, wished to marry you." She smiled at him. "I need not fear for my financial stability. Father has amply provided for me as those documents attest. I am at liberty to choose a match based on compatibility and, if I am so fortunate, love. And you might pursue such a match for yourself without scorn or derision from society as I am the one to call off this sham of an engagement."

Darcy sat slack-jawed, unable to know where to begin a reply to such a declaration, but Anne was not yet through.

"I believe I might be of assistance to you in finding ladies who would suit your temperament, but I will need you to place your trust in me." She placed her glass on the table and leaned toward Darcy. "I have studied your character for years, Fitzwilliam. I believe I am as qualified as you, if not more qualified, to find an acceptable match for you."

"You..." He shook his head to clear away the fog. "You will find a match for me?"

"Indeed I will, but first I must inform Mother of my decision to not marry you." Anne stood and walked to the window that looked out over the park toward the parsonage at Hunsford. "Mother has a new parson. Did you know?"

Darcy nodded. "Yes, I have met him. He was visiting relatives in Hertfordshire when I was there with Bingley."

"He was sent to find a wife from amongst his cousins." She watched Darcy's face discretely and bit back a smile at the horror that passed across his features. "He was successful in finding a wife...." She turned and paused purposefully. "They were married in January." The colour had drained completely from his face, and she wondered for a moment if she had gone too far in ascertaining the truth of Mrs. Collins' words regarding his feelings. They had shared many fascinating conversations regarding Darcy's stay in Hertfordshire. "It is unfortunate he did not choose to marry one of his cousins as such a marriage would have been to the family's advantage, what with the entail and all."

Darcy slumped forward and rested his head in his hands. "He did not marry a cousin?"

"No." Anne came to sit near him once more. "He married Miss Lucas. I assume you know of whom I speak. I have been given to understand her father is well-known in Hertfordshire." She studied how his shoulders relaxed and noticed him rub at the corner of one eye. She placed a hand on his shoulder and whispered. "The lady who is your heart's desire remains unattached." His body tensed under her touch, and she was certain his breathing had ceased. "Mrs Collins is her particular friend, it seems, and she, along with Mrs. Collin's sister, has come to stay at the parsonage for a visit. She has been here a fortnight, and I find I shall quite miss her when she leaves. So open and welcoming. Intelligent, too. It is through her I discovered just how much damage my mother's tales of our engagement might be causing." She withdrew her hand from his shoulder and sat back in her chair, waiting for his reaction.

"Elizabeth is here?" He whispered.

Anne smiled to herself. He was clearly more smitten than even Mrs Collins realized, and certainly more than Elizabeth would consider. "She is, and she is under the impression we are to marry should you ever be a gentleman and ask me."

Darcy looked at Anne, his brows furrowed. "How has she heard this? She does not circulate amongst the ton."

"Her cousin made mention of it to her as did another gentleman — although I fear that label is a misnomer for a man such as Mr. Wickham. I believe it is he who called your honour into question, and it is not the only lie he has told her regarding you."

"And she believed him?" Darcy was clearly angry.

"And why should she not? You were less than civil, and he is all that is charming. Your dour facade makes it easy for him to convince others of your harshness."

Darcy was on his feet and pacing the room. "But she is not a silly woman like her mother and sisters. She is intelligent. You said so yourself. Why would she believe him?"

Anne began to feel a bit of trepidation. She had not expected him to react well, but his outburst was so uncharacteristic of him that it was unsettling. "She looks to find fault in you."

"Why?" Agony rang in his voice and marred his handsome features.

"According to Mrs Collins, who knows her far better than I, she fights against an attraction to you."

"That makes no sense." He threw his hands up in exasperation.

"It truly makes no sense?" Anne found a small amount of annoyance at his obtuseness creeping into her mind. Did he really have no idea of the charges the young woman had against him? She had been shocked at many of the things Mrs. Collins had told her about her cousin's behaviour. True, it had been told to her through the perspective of a person who was a dear friend of the offended and privy to her personal opinion, but based on her knowledge of Mrs. Collins, the woman did not disseminate misrepresentations. The information had been told to her in confidence with a hope toward the happy resolution of the situation left unresolved when Darcy had so suddenly departed Netherfield. Perhaps he needed to be made aware of just how much his pride had harmed his chances with the lady who so obviously held his heart.

"Did you not slight her at a public assembly? Did you not direct your friend to not return to Netherfield? Why did you do these things? Because you truly found her merely tolerable? Because her family — a gentleman's family — was beneath the standing of a friend who had recently been in trade? Or was it because you were looking to find fault so that you might fight your attraction to her?"

She stood in front of him and jabbed his chest with her finger as she asked each question.

Anne turned and walked away from him. "She is not of the first circles. She has only a small dowry, and she has, by her own admission, embarrassingly ill-mannered relations as well as some who are in trade. But, she is a gentleman's daughter, and you are a gentleman's son. On that, you are equals. You have no need of her dowry, and you possess your own share of ill-mannered relations though they are of the first circles and are not so closely related to trade. Your pride does not serve you well in this instance, Fitzwilliam."

Anne stood again at the window. "She has already been called upon by several young men in the area, and she has just met our cousin. They seem to be falling into conversation easily." Darcy was beside her at the window. "She will never consider you if you do not put away your pride and appear to be human." She gave him a jab in the side with her elbow. "And she will never consider you if she believes you are promised to another because she has far too much integrity to do so." Anne took his arm and led him away from the window and toward the door of the sitting room. "Now, she was to visit with me this afternoon, but I have a very important discussion to have with my mother, and I would greatly appreciate your assistance in keeping her occupied and out of doors while my mother throws her fit."

"But will you not need me?"

"No, I would rather that you not be here. However, if you would not mind, could you ask Richard to join me?" She smiled archly at him. "Please extend my regrets to Miss Bennet for not being able to keep our appointment. You will see that she is safely returned to Mrs. Collins, will you not?"

Anne gave him a firm push out the door and then closed it behind him before he could find a reason to ignore her directives. She crossed to the window once again and looking down, caught Richard's eye and waved. He gave a nod of his head and looked toward the door just as Darcy exited.

~*~*~*~*~*~

Richard offered his arm to Elizabeth and lead her toward the small garden on the side of the house. He coughed to keep from laughing as he saw his cousin nearly run towards them.

"I fear our conversation is about to be interrupted, Miss Bennet." He slowed to a stop as he heard Darcy call his name. "It seems my cousin has need of me."

"Mr. Darcy is your cousin?" asked Elizabeth. Richard coughed again to cover a chuckle. He noted how the lady at his side did not have to turn to know that it was Darcy who called him.

"He is indeed." Richard turned as Darcy drew near.

"Miss Bennet." Darcy bowed slightly in greeting.

"Mr. Darcy." She inclined her head in acknowledgement.

"Was there a reason for your interruption? I was having a most pleasant conversation with Miss Bennet." He bit the inside of his cheek. It was difficult not to give in to the mirth which consumed him at the way his staid cousin blinked in confusion.

"I…uh…that is, Anne requested your presence."

"And I am her servant whom she calls, and I must answer?"

Elizabeth gasped.

"Richard!" chided Darcy. "She has asked you for your help. She does not demand your presence."

"Yes, she is not her mother."

"Richard!" Darcy took a step towards him. "She needs your assistance."

"Why? Why does she need my assistance?" Richard feigned ignorance.

"She has matters to discuss with her mother concerning her future."

"Ah. Your engagement." Richard congratulated himself on getting to his objective of leaving his cousin and Miss Bennet with something about which to speak. He knew Darcy would not bring up such a subject on his own, and he was equally as certain that Miss Bennet was too polite a lady to broach the subject. What his cousin needed was a friendly nudge in the right direction.

Darcy's eyes narrowed.

"She has finally refused you?"

"That would imply an offer." Darcy nearly growled at Richard. Had Elizabeth not been present, Richard was sure he would have received a well-deserved and colourful set down.

"You know as well as I, Aunt Catherine will perceive Anne's position as a refusal."

"Which is precisely why she requests your presence."

"But why Colonel Fitzwilliam's presence and not yours?" Elizabeth coloured. "Forgive me. I had not intended to say that aloud."

A smile spread across Richard's face as he bowed to take his leave. "That is a good question, Miss Bennet. I shall leave Darcy to attempt the answer; however, should I survive this foray into enemy territory, and you find his answer inadequate, I shall do my best to assist you."

"No, truly, Colonel. It is not for me to know. I should not have asked."

Richard winked at her. "Ah, but I believe it is for you to know." He stepped close to Darcy and muttered softly. "Use your chance wisely, or you will leave me no option but to reveal all I know of your feelings."

Chapter 2

"Oh, thank heavens, you are here." Anne stopped pacing. "I was certain that mother was going to get here before you. Whatever took you so long? Did Darcy not tell you I needed you? Did you not remember that you were to leave Darcy alone with Miss Bennet?"

Richard slowly poured himself a drink and sauntered to the window before replying. "I came as quickly as I was able. I needed to ensure our taciturn cousin and the lovely Miss Bennet had a topic for conversation."

Anne groaned. "I would ask what the topic is, but I fear I do not have time to calm myself before my mother appears."

"I do not know why you do not place more faith in my tactics. I am a trained colonel in His Majesty's army. I have led many campaigns."

Anne sighed. "And did all your men return — unharmed?"

"Of course not! The goal is to limit casualties, but it is nigh unto impossible to come away completely unscathed." He stretched his legs out in front of him and crossed his ankles. "My numbers for casualties were always low — well within acceptable limits."

"And what is the acceptable limit to the battle which might be playing out in my garden?"

"Battle? That is not a battle. That is Darcy explaining himself to a lady."

Anne tapped her fingers on the arm of her chair and raised an eyebrow as she stared at Richard. Finally, his eyes grew wide. "You did not account for the inability of your soldier to use the weapon of well-formulated thoughts, now did you?"

Richard closed his eyes as if in agony. "I forgot he cannot speak to ladies as eloquently as he can to me or Bingley. But surely with the topic of your engagement already broached, the remaining explanation should not be outside his capabilities." Richard looked at Anne hopefully.

"I would not wager on that." Anne shook her head. "It is no wonder we still have wars with men in charge. I do hope you perform more admirably in a few moments. I shall need your support. This battle will not be easily won." She inclined her head toward the door and placed a finger on her lips.

Richard listened. There was a faint clacking sound that grew louder.

"It is fortunate she insists on such noisy shoes," Anne

whispered. A moment later the door to Anne's sitting room opened, and Lady Catherine bustled in.

"Are you well?" She went to Anne and laid a hand on her forehead.

Anne pushed her mother's hand away gently. "I am well, Mother."

Lady Catherine's eyes narrowed as she studied her daughter. "Then why did you send for me?"

"Can a daughter not send for her mother without being ill?"

"She can, but you do not."

"Please, Mother, be seated. I have something I wish to discuss with you." Anne waited while her mother took a seat next to Richard.

"And why are you here, Richard? Should you not be surveying the park or exercising a horse?"

"I was, and I will. But, Anne has asked me to attend her for this meeting as it has to do with her future, and you know Uncle Louis insisted that my father, my brother or myself be privy to such discussions whether in person or through post."

Lady Catherine squared her shoulders and raised her eyebrows. "Her future is with Darcy. I see no need to discuss anything other than the time and place of the nuptials. Your father will see to the settlement papers though I expect Darcy to be most generous and thorough."

"My future is for me to decide, not you, not Darcy, not even Uncle Henry," said Anne.

"Your future has already been decided. There is nothing to discuss." Lady Catherine began to rise from her chair.

"I will not marry Darcy." Anne's voice was firm.

Lady Catherine dropped back into her chair. "What are you saying? You will marry Darcy. It has been arranged."

"No, Mother, it has not." Anne rose and walked to her writing desk. She withdrew a packet of papers from the drawer and handed them to Richard. "Richard, what are these papers?"

Richard unfolded them. "They appear to be marriage papers with your name on them."

Lady Catherine's eyes grew large, and she placed a hand on her heart. "What have you done?" She demanded.

"Anne has done nothing, Aunt. These were written by her father."

Lady Catherine snatched the papers from Richard. "It cannot be. They were..." Her voice trailed off. She flipped through the documents. "It simply cannot be. Who has fabricated this...this....deception?" She stood and waved the papers in front of Richard. "Did you do this? Or your father? He always was a scheming man! Arranging and manipulating!"

Lady Catherine turned to Anne. "These are worthless forgeries." She tossed the papers into the fireplace and watched them catch. "You will marry Darcy. I shall see to it!"

Richard stood at the door blocking her exit. "No, you will not. My uncle's wishes will be fulfilled, and you will not stand in the way."

"Who shall stop me? You have no proof of his wishes. They are but sparks on the wind." She sneered at him. "My Anne shall not be passed about the drawing rooms of London."

"Then I shall marry from Hunsford." Anne stepped between her mother and cousin.

"You shall marry Darcy!"

"I shall not! It was not Father's wish!"

"And just what was your father's wish? I see no father here to state his desires for you. I see no papers containing them. What is a daughter to a father that he should care for her future unless it increases his wealth?"

Anne took a step forward causing her mother to retreat a step. "My father loved me and has provided for me. He wished for me to find love, not to marry just for wealth and position as he did." She stepped forward again, and her mother once again retreated. "And you, you who should love me dearly, have tried to keep his gift from me." She poked at her mother's chest. "You would see me unhappy."

"Unhappy? How could you be unhappy? Darcy is all that is good and respectable. He would never use you ill. You would be well provided for — you would want for nothing."

"Nothing but love." Anne's fists were balled tightly at her side. "Darcy cares for me as a cousin ought but not as a husband should. Of this, you are fully aware. You know he is respectable, and you circulate a fabrication of an engagement knowing he will not discredit you and bring shame to our family. You take from him any chance of happiness. How could you?" Anne turned away from her mother in disgust. "Richard, please inform my mother of how my future will be decided. I find I do not wish to speak to her further." Anne returned to her chair and glowered at her mother but remained silent.

Richard cleared his throat and motioned for his aunt to take a seat. Slowly he removed a packet of papers from his pocket. "We expected you to destroy the copies of your husband's wishes. You will find that this is also a copy. The originals, which have been read by myself, my father, my brother, and Darcy, are safely stored."

Richard unfolded the documents. "Anne has been left a tidy sum of money that shall be given to her when she turns five and twenty. Rosings will remain in your custody until such a time as Anne secures a husband who is in want of an estate — as stipulated by her father — then it shall be given to him. As I am sure you are aware, you shall not have any say in whom your daughter marries. The honour of granting permission to marry — necessary not because of Anne's age but because of inheritance of Rosings that will be passed on — has been bestowed upon myself and Darcy."

He flipped through the papers. "There are a few other stipulations, but they are of little concern to you." His finger slid over the paragraphs. "Except for this one. It is advised, though the final decision is left to Anne alone, that she looks for a husband outside of London — in deference to her mother — whatever that might mean." He raised an eyebrow and peered over the papers at his aunt. To his surprise, she looked down at her hands, and he was certain a blush crept across her cheeks. He had never seen her show any emotion other than irritation, worry or anger.

Finally, she spoke in a resigned voice. "So that is it? I am to have no say in my daughter's marriage?"

"That appears to be the case," confirmed Richard. "However, if Anne were to request your advice and guidance, you might have at least a token say."

Lady Catherine looked hopefully to her daughter.

"No." Anne shook her head slowly. "You have lost my trust. You should have looked out for my happiness, but you did not."

"Anne,..." began her mother.

Anne rose and opened the door. "I believe our meeting

is at an end. Perhaps I shall be willing to listen to you in the future, but I find I cannot just yet."

Lady Catherine rose slowly. She lifted her chin and pulled her shoulders back. She paused at the door. "I always had your wellbeing in mind."

Anne closed the door softly behind her mother and rested her head against it.

"Are you well?" Richard placed a hand on her shoulder.

Anne turned and gave him a weak smile. "Growth is never free of pain, is it?"

Richard nodded a greeting to Mrs. Jenkins, who slipped back into the room and took up the stitching she had abandoned when Lady Catherine had arrived for her meeting. She looked nervously at her charge.

Anne smiled reassuringly at the woman who had been with her since childhood. "It went as expected. Mother is not pleased, but she seems subdued." She turned to the window. "But, I wish to think on more pleasant topics." Her eyes searched the garden, trying to catch even a glimpse of her cousin and Miss Elizabeth, but she could not.

Richard came to stand next to her. "Might you like to take a turn about the garden, Anne?"

"I will get my wrap and bonnet." Anne hurried from the room and met her cousin in the garden. They walked along in companionable silence for a while. Anne drew in several refreshing breaths of crisp spring air. The fragrance of freshly turned earth and early spring flowers was soothing to her.

"Insufferable man!" Elizabeth muttered as she stepped onto the path near where Anne and Richard walked. She was so immersed in her own thoughts she did not notice them until she nearly ran into Richard.

She blushed and stammered an apology, keeping her eyes on the ground, but a small sniffle gave away the fact that she was quite distraught. Mrs. Jenkins placed an arm around her and led her to a nearby stone bench.

"I believe I must find our ineloquent cousin," whispered Richard.

Anne lifted an accusatory eyebrow at him.

"I know. I am sorry."

Anne took a seat near Elizabeth. It was silent save for a few sniffles and the chirping of the birds for several minutes.

"Did you truly ask him not to attend you when you spoke to your mother?" Elizabeth spoke barely above a whisper.

"Yes."

"Oh." Elizabeth twisted her handkerchief.

"You did not believe him?" asked Anne.

Elizabeth shook her head and a small hiccup of a sob escaped her.

"It made him angry." Anne sighed. "He prides himself on being above disguise."

Elizabeth nodded. "A modicum of disguise may have served him better than abject honesty."

"Oh, dear," said Anne as she placed an arm about Elizabeth's shoulder. "He can be unbearable when his pride is wounded. What did he say?"

Elizabeth shook her head. "I knew that I was beneath his notice, that he found me merely tolerable, but to abuse me so. It is insupportable!" She stood and began pacing. "I have no illusions that my family is above reproach. I am fully aware of their shortcomings. I do not need them to be laid before me!" She stamped her foot and wrapped her arms around herself. "Arrogant, arrogant man!"

"He spoke ill of your family?" Anne asked in astonishment.

"Indeed he did. My mother, my sisters, even my father!" Elizabeth's voice wavered. "And what he has done to Jane…" She covered her face with her hands. "It is unforgivable." She uncovered her face and dried her eyes before turning to Anne. "I am sorry. I must go. It is not right for me to be so open with my feelings." She gasped. "Perhaps he is right. I am all that is improper." Elizabeth sat heavily on the bench.

"Improper?" Shock suffused Anne's face. "He did not say you were improper? He could not, for you are no such thing!"

Elizabeth shook her head. "No, he did not say I was improper, but he did say Lydia was, and here I sit acting as she would." She let out a long slow breath. "I must go. Charlotte will be expecting me soon."

Anne placed a hand on Elizabeth's arm. "You must not return to the parsonage in such a state. Think of your cousin." Anne stood. She knew that if Mr. Collins were to see his cousin, there would be questions and lectures. It was not something that anyone should be subjected to, let alone a young woman who was so terribly distraught. "No, I insist you remain here until evening. We are all to dine together. I shall simply send a note informing Charlotte that you will not be returning this afternoon and to send you whatever you may need to prepare for dinner."

"But Mr. Darcy." Elizabeth's voice was filled with panic. "I cannot see him. I simply cannot."

"You can, and you will." Anne commanded. "He must be made to deal with the pain he has inflicted, but fear not, I shall not leave you all evening. You are to be my constant companion. Together we will weather the storms caused by your Mr. Darcy and my mother."

"He is not now nor shall he ever be my Mr. Darcy," Elizabeth replied emphatically.

Anne lifted her eyebrows, a small smile pulling at the corners of her mouth. "If you say so, my dear. Now, we should return to the house before my cousins find us."

Chapter 3

Richard took a last look at the lovely Miss Elizabeth, who was dissolving into tears on the bench next to Mrs. Jenkins. He shook his head. How had a simple explanation of a supposed engagement gone so painfully wrong? He headed toward the stables. He knew his cousin would wish to ride away his troubles.

"Darcy!" he called as he neared the stables where Darcy stood waiting for a groom to bring his horse.

"Go away, Richard," Darcy growled.

"No." Richard grabbed Darcy by the arm and started propelling him away from the stables.

Darcy pulled his arm, trying to extricate it from Richard's hold. "Richard, I am going riding."

"You are not dressed for it. The fit of your jacket alone will surely make you regret the ride later if you go as you are."

"I am going riding," Darcy growled. He broadened his stance, making it harder for his cousin to pull him from his spot.

"No, you are not." Richard's tone had turned hard. He glared at his cousin and tightened his grip on Darcy's arm. "We need to talk."

"I do not wish to talk." Darcy once again tried to pull his arm from Richard's grip.

"That does not signify."

"Remove your hand from my person."

"I will not until you have agreed to come with me and talk."

Darcy scowled at Richard. "I shall agree to no such thing, and you will remove your hand."

Richard noted Darcy's balled fist and released Darcy's arm. "Go ahead. Take a swing at me. See if that lessens the pain and anger you feel or increases it." He braced himself as he watched Darcy's eyes flash. "I shall not stop you. You have my leave to hit me." He clasped his hands behind his back.

Darcy glowered at him for a moment longer before turning away. "I do not wish to harm you."

Richard took a step closer so that his chest nearly touched Darcy's shoulder. "But you do wish to harm someone. Who? And why?"

Darcy glanced over his shoulder and took a step away from his cousin. "I do not wish to speak of it. Leave me."

"I will not, and you know it." Richard stepped closer once again.

Darcy's shoulders sagged. "Can you not let me ride?"

"Ha. Leave you alone when you are in such a state? I think not." Richard crossed his arms over his chest. "I did that last summer, and do you remember how that ended?" Richard thought of the state in which he found his cousin after George Wickham's attempted seduction of Darcy's sister, Georgiana.

It had been a fearful sight to behold! His steadfast, composed cousin had a split lip and black eye from one too many sessions at Gentleman Jackson's, smelled strongly of alcohol, and appeared to have been wearing the same clothes for days. Richard knew that his cousin's uncharacteristic behaviour was an attempt to rid himself of the guilt he felt over not protecting his sister — an unfounded guilt. His cousin had a penchant for feeling the weight of errors more deeply than most.

"This is not the same," protested Darcy.

Richard laughed. "You are right. Your guilt last summer was misplaced."

Darcy grimaced.

"Today, I would venture to guess the lion's share of the guilt should rest firmly on your shoulders. I will not let you avoid it, nor will I help you destroy yourself because of it." Richard placed a hand on Darcy's shoulder. "Come. We will walk, and you will talk. Then, we will decide how you are to right your wrongs without doing harm to your person."

~*~*~*~*~*~

Three hours later it was a calmer Darcy and a less emotional Elizabeth that entered the dining room at Rosings. Tonight, Mr. and Mrs. Collins as well as Mr. and Mrs. Martin Barrows of Ravinwood Manor, their younger son Mr. Christopher Barrows, and his sister Miss Abigail Barrows were in attendance.

Anne's nerves were on edge as she watched her mother take her seat at the far end of the table. She hoped that her mother would hold her tongue and not let any comment slip regarding their disagreement. It would not be an obvious comment; her mother was too well-bred to air grievances in front of guests, but she was skilled at the covert jibe — a raised brow, a slight inflection, an added emphasis to a word here and there. Anne had observed and endured it for years. There was always some sort of disparagement that her mother would impart in such a fashion when in company. But, tonight she feared that the majority of this ridicule would fall on her instead of their guests.

To add to her discomfort, she knew that Mrs. Barrows was not ignorant of her mother's methods of censure. They had been friends for many years, both having come out in the same season and being fortunate enough to have married men of wealth whose estates were situated so near each other.

Anne smiled through dinner, keeping Miss Elizabeth occupied with conversation and doing her best to ignore the particular inflection that her mother was placing on the word disappointment tonight. Indeed, it was amazing how many times her mother had managed to work that one word into every conversation she had. Had she not been the source of the disappointment, she might have been impressed by her mother's skill, but as it was, she only felt its sting.

"Miss de Bourgh," said Charlotte quietly as they rose to retire to the drawing room. "Might I have a word?"

Anne gave a slight nod and led Charlotte to one of three alcoves in the room.

"I was watching Elizabeth during dinner. She does not seem herself. She pushed her food about her plate; her eyes only left their downward gaze when spoken to directly; and she never truly entered into any conversation — there was no debate, no levity — it is quite unlike her. Is she well? I would ask her, but I know she shall say she is well, even if she is not."

Anne glanced about her. She took note of how Elizabeth sat silently near Miss Barrow, who was in animated conversation. "Her spirits are low." Anne sighed. "Much has transpired this afternoon and not all of it — well, nearly none of it actually — has been pleasant." Anne dropped her voice to be even softer. "I spoke to my mother of my father's wishes. While I spoke to her, Colonel Fitzwilliam and I arranged for Mr. Darcy to walk with Elizabeth in the garden. We had hoped he would explain about his supposed engagement to me."

Charlotte placed a hand on Anne's arm. "They argued?"

Anne nodded. "I am afraid they did. Injurious words were spoken on both sides, and it took the better part of the afternoon to calm them. Instead of securing their happiness, which was our plan, it seems we have been the cause of great agony."

"But they are calm now," said Charlotte with a smile. "That means Elizabeth is now in the process of evaluating her words, and her silence means she is seeing her own errors. We need but a small opportunity for apology, and happiness will be back within the realm of possibility."

Anne furrowed her brow. "Are you certain?"

Charlotte laughed softly. "It is how she has always behaved. Her anger or hurt often overtake her sense and her tongue. I have witnessed it — nay, even been a recipient of it — on more than one occasion. At home, she would wander off into the wilderness and then return with her sense restored and repentance on her lips."

"But we are in company." Anne looked about at the number gathered. "The gentlemen shall rejoin us shortly, but I do not see how we can provide for such an opportunity with so many gathered. And my mother, should she suspect what is happening —."

"Anne, of what are you and Mrs Collins speaking? I must know. It is quite disappointing to be excluded from conversation." Lady Catherine called.

Anne turned and smiled as sweetly as she could at her mother. "Pray forgive us. It is but a trivial and personal matter. I assure you we were not sharing secrets of great significance." She bit back a smile of triumph as she watched her mother's eyes narrow slightly.

"Oh," said Miss Barrows as if she had suddenly been poked with a stick. "Miss de Bourgh, could we not play a parlour game? The gentlemen shall be joining us soon, and if we do not entertain them with music or games, they shall wander off again to find their own amusements, and conversation is ever so much more pleasant when there are gentlemen involved."

Anne gave the young lady an appraising look. It had not escaped her notice how Miss Barrows batted her eyes at both of her cousins. "Perhaps you could take a turn on the pianoforte so that the music will draw them into the room, and then we can discuss the possibility of games."

Miss Barrows fairly glowed with pleasure. "Oh, but I know the exact game we should play."

"I do not play games," said Lady Catherine.

"Yes," agreed Mrs. Barrows. "It would be much more sensible to just entertain with music, my dear."

Anne noted the small pout that started to form on Miss Barrows' lips and felt Charlotte's light pat on her arm.

"Miss de Bourgh," said Charlotte. "Could not those who wish to play a game gather on the far side of the room, while those of us who do not remain here. I am sure my husband will be happy to have me play for him, and then we shall have both music and games?" She gave Anne a significant look.

"Mrs. Collins, that is an excellent idea!" Anne stood. "Miss Barrows, you shall take your turn at the instrument first. Then, we shall play your game while Mrs. Collins has her turn. Perhaps afterwards?, you might exhibit for us some more?" This last comment brought a pleased smile to Mrs. Barrows' face. Obviously, the girl's mother was eager s to have her daughter brought to the attention of one and all.

Miss Barrows took her turn on the pianoforte as the gentlemen entered the room and found their places in one of the two groups. Darcy hesitated in his decision for a moment until Richard pointed out refusing to play games meant an extended conversation with not only his aunt but also her parson. So it was that Darcy took his seat in the game circle.

"Abigail," said her brother. "I have saved you a seat." He moved one chair away from Darcy as he stood to extend his hand to his sister.

Richard fought the urge to roll his eyes at such an obvious tactic. "And what is the game you wish to play, Miss Barrows?" he asked.

"Oh, it is called Three Wishes."

"I have not heard of that game," said Richard.

"Oh, no, you would not have for it is a game that my school friends and I created. It is ever such a good way to learn about people." She smiled at him.

"Then, you must inform us of the rules."

Miss Barrows sat a bit straighter and lifted her chin. "We shall go about the circle and each person will share a wish. The first go round we may only wish for something to give to another. On your second turn, you must only wish for some object for yourself. Your third wish must be a character wish. You must wish for one thing which you think is lacking in your character. I shall start, then my brother, then Miss de Bourgh and so on until we have completed the circle and begin again." She glanced around to see if there were any remaining questions before she began.

~*~*~*~*~*~

"Miss Bennet, it is your turn," said Miss Barrows on the third pass around the circle. "You must tell us a character wish."

Elizabeth lifted her eyes and smiled at Miss Barrows. "I wish for my sister's serenity and gentleness of spirit."

"You must explain why," prompted Miss Barrows.

"I lack a calmness of spirit. I wish for the ability to keep my emotions under regulation at all times."

"But would it not then be difficult for others to know what you are feeling? Surely too much serenity could lead to difficulties of misunderstanding," Miss Barrows questioned.

"It may," replied Elizabeth. "It may also lead to disappointment, but a lack of peace coupled with a spirit lacking in gentleness can lead to a far greater amount of pain. I have often become overwrought, and I can assure you that doing so can lead to hurt and shame."

"Shame?"

"Yes, Miss Barrows. One tends to feel shame when one has spoken without thought and with unbridled passion."

Miss Barrows opened her mouth to question further, but Richard swiftly moved in and shared his character wish.

"Mr. Darcy," said Miss Barrows sweetly. "What is your character wish?"

"You may be asking too much of my cousin, Miss Barrows," said Richard. "He is a man who has few character flaws." Richard gave his cousin a teasing smile.

Darcy scowled at him. "My cousin jests. I have many flaws. There is not one of us perfect, but he is correct in that sharing such flaws is not something I do easily. Perhaps that should be my wish."

"Is it your wish, Mr. Darcy?" asked Miss Barrows.

He shook his head. "No, my wish is for eloquence."

"Eloquence?" said several in unison.

Darcy nodded.

"But, Darcy," said Richard, "I have heard your ability

to instruct your steward; I have heard you debate many a complex topic with my father; and I cannot say with good conscience that you lack in eloquence. Unless you have a plausible explanation for your choice, you will have to make another wish."

"I do not speak of an eloquence of thought. I speak of an eloquence of the heart. What you have said is true. I have a vast amount of knowledge gleaned from years of learning, and I do possess the ability to debate and instruct, but I lack the ability possessed by the poet. I cannot speak things as I feel them. Indeed, I often lack the ability to listen to my heart." He shifted his gaze from Richard to Elizabeth. "And this lack of ability has led me, on more than one occasion, to injure those I love."

Richard cleared his throat. "Yes, well, I withdraw my objection. Your wish is valid, Darcy." He leaned a bit forward both to look around his cousin to Miss Barrows and to hopefully afford Elizabeth some measure of privacy. "Miss Barrows, did I hear you were scheduled to entertain us with your musical abilities? If so, might I escort you to the instrument?" He stood and offered her his arm.

"Miss Bennet?" Anne leaned a bit closer. "I believe I should very much like to take a stroll to the library. Would you be so kind as to accompany me?"

Elizabeth tore her eyes away from Mr. Darcy. "It would be my pleasure, Miss de Bourgh."

"Darcy, your arm would be a most welcome support." Anne rose and stood expectantly before her cousin.

"Of course." He looked to Elizabeth. "I have two arms."

Elizabeth blushed but placed her hand on his free arm. The threesome proceeded to make a turn about the sitting room before exiting through the far door as Richard made a show of helping Miss Barrows get situated at the instrument.

Anne dropped Darcy's arm as soon as they had reached the library and found a single chair tucked away in a tight corner. She picked up a book from the small round table which stood next to the chair. "Darcy," she cautioned. "Choose your words wisely for I shall not afford you another moment of privacy with Miss Bennet if you upset her again." She waited for him to give a nod of acknowledgement before turning her attention to her book.

Anne bent her head over the book, but her eyes followed the progression of Darcy and Elizabeth as they moved to a nearby seating area. She strained to hear their lowered voices.

"Mr. Darcy," began Elizabeth. "I must apologize for my intemperate speech earlier today. I allowed –."

"Your head to be controlled by your heart. That is not something for which you need apologize," Darcy interrupted.

"I, on the other hand, tried to control my heart with

my head. That is by far a more grievous offence. My sentiments were not expressed as they should have been." He looked down at his hands, which were nervously rubbing small circles on his knees.

Elizabeth placed her hands on his to stop their motion. "My heart has pondered your words, and I believe it has finally heard what you were attempting to say."

Anne turned an unread page and shifted slightly in her chair.

"Despite your misgivings, despite your machinations to rid your life of all evidence of me, you could not, for your heart would not allow it."

Darcy grasped her hands in his. "I know you have little reason to think highly of me. I have behaved abominably."

"And I have not?" Elizabeth asked. "I, who willingly, determinedly believed the worst of you without evidence?" She shook her head. "We have both behaved in a shameful fashion. You have been proud, and I have been prejudiced. Neither of us has much good to recommend ourselves to the other. We must begin again."

"I should like that, but there are words which were spoken that must be addressed."

Elizabeth sighed. "You are right. There are matters we must necessarily discuss, but perhaps we will do so with a better understanding of the other."

"But not tonight. Tonight I only wish to know that you are willing to consider me. Have I any hope of success?"

Anne held her breath and stilled the page she was about to turn as she listened for Elizabeth's reply. An impertinent smile graced her friend's face, and a twinkle of mischief shone in her eye. Anne released her breath and flipped the page.

"I have no doubt you are successful in most things, are you not, Mr. Darcy?" She raised a brow and tilted her head slightly, giving him a playful look. "I have no reason to believe you shall not also succeed in this."

Richard slipped into the library and approached Anne from behind. He smiled as he saw Elizabeth blush slightly when his cousin kissed each of her hands. He gingerly grasped the little curl that always hung in front of Anne's ear and gave it a slight pull. Anne jumped and let out a little squeal.

"Your mother is beginning to question your disappearance and longing for Miss Bennet to exhibit. I believe she grows tired of Miss Barrows' limited repertoire."

Anne snapped her book shut. "That is no reason to disturb my reading in such a fashion."

Richard chuckled softly. "Reading?" He reached down and took the book from her hands, turning it right ways up before returning it to her. Anne's cheeks flushed a brilliant shade of crimson, and she quickly laid the book on the table.

"Come," said Richard taking her hand. "We must

return without delay." He helped her to her feet and tucked her hand in the crook of his arm.

Chapter 4

Anne cradled her teacup in her hands, warming them. She inhaled deeply of the fragrance. To her, there was more comfort to be found in a simple cup of tea than the mere drinking of it. It was an experience to be savoured, and this first cup in the morning served as a source of pleasure and a time of reflection.

Yesterday had been a series of emotional events. By the time she had retired to her suite last evening, Anne had been a weary mass of raw, exposed nerves. She was surprised and not a little relieved when she woke this morning without an ache or pain — no headache, no stiff muscles, no nausea. She sighed. It was an exhalation of peace. She had never felt so at ease in her own home as she did this day. A small portion of her mind taunted her that such a feeling could not last, and, indeed, she knew that it would not. Her mother would soon make her presence known, and Anne could not deceive herself enough to think her mother would have miraculously turned into a caring, doting mother, full of understanding and support for a daughter who, though now in charge of her future, felt trepidation as she faced it. Upon hearing footsteps in the hall, she straightened in her chair and placed the cup on the table.

"Good morning, Richard," she said without turning to see who had entered.

A low chuckle rumbled near her ear as he bent to kiss her cheek, something he had done all his life when first greeting her in the morning on his visits to Rosings.

"Hmmm," he said as he straightened. "Perhaps it is no longer proper for me to greet you thusly now that you are no longer betrothed to my cousin."

Anne swatted his arm. "I have never been betrothed to our cousin. There is no need to change your actions just because my mother has finally been made to accept reality."

"Tongues could wag, making it harder for you to find a husband." He gathered a roll and coffee from the sideboard.

She stared at his broad shoulders, noting how his jacket stretched and relaxed as he moved. "Perhaps you are right." She took a small bite of her toast and chewed slowly, contemplating her cousin's words.

"I was teasing." He settled into the chair on her right. It was where he always sat to break his fast with her.

"Yes, I know. But the business of finding a husband will not be easy. Had I started at a younger age, it might have been a small matter, but I am so old, quite past my prime, perhaps my bloom has faded."

Richard laughed aloud at her comment. "You, my dear, are not old, nor has your beauty faded. You are as beautiful today as you were at a proper coming-out age. You are wiser and more sensible than the average young lady making her debut, but you are no less desirable."

Anne smiled at him for his solicitous words. He truly was a very loving and supportive cousin. He had spent the whole of the evening after their return from the library at her side, fending off comments from her mother and shielding her from the advances of Mr. Barrows.

She inclined her head in acceptance of his words. "You speak as a dutiful cousin should, and I thank you for it."

Richard shook his head firmly. "No, no. I do not speak to fulfill a duty, Anne. It is the truth. I have seen the debutantes in the ballrooms this season, and few compare to you." He took a sip of his coffee before continuing. "And those who succeed in approaching your beauty lack sense. In truth, many seem to have feathers for brains. I assure you, were you to come to London, you would always have a full dance card and an equally full drawing room."

Anne laughed lightly, and her cheeks flushing at such effusions. She knew Richard was not a man to tell tales or choose his words to spare another's feelings.

"Thank you," she said softly. "But, I shall not be going

to town. I must settle for the few gentlemen I might find here."

Richard smiled mischievously at her. "You could accept Mr. Barrows and save yourself the bother of searching. He seemed eager enough to please last evening."

Anne groaned. "If I did not know better, I would think he had learned of my circumstances and was doing his best to acquire an estate. He was most complimentary of mother, the furnishings, the artwork, the pianoforte, and on and on, but he had not one word of compliment toward my person or my abilities." She rose and walked to the window. "His mother is also my mother's dearest friend. I could not be tied to two such similar women."

Richard came to stand near her. He leaned casually against the wall next to the window, coffee cup in hand. "It may be best to keep the details of your father's documents secret until you have secured a man's heart. Many are without scruples when it comes to acquiring wealth and land. More than one young lady has found herself tied to misery for the sake of what she brings in the way of wealth to a marriage." He shifted slightly, so that he could see the walkway outside the window better. "My brother's wife would not hesitate to lend her agreement to such a statement. The money she brought with her is gone, gambled away. I do not know the particulars of their relationship, but they each do their best to avoid the other." He looked sadly at Anne. "It is not an existence I would wish on anyone, but especially not you. I could not bear to know you were so ill-used."

Anne laid a hand on his arm. "And that is why I am so pleased Father has appointed you and Fitzwilliam in his stead. I know you both have my best interest in mind, just as he did."

"Speaking of Darcy." Richard nodded toward the window as he took a gulp of his coffee. "He is looking rather happy after his walk this morning. I assume he met with his lovely lady on his rounds."

"I am sure he did. As she was preparing to leave last evening, I heard him telling her where he might be walking this morning and at what time." She turned to return to the table. "I am happy for him."

"As am I, though I will miss the camaraderie we have enjoyed over the years. Wife and family will change that."

"He has not secured her yet," Anne cautioned.

"Oh, but he will. What father would refuse the Master of Pemberley?"

"A father who supported his daughter's decision to refuse the proposal of her cousin and heir to the family estate."

Richard's brows rose. "But surely if the daughter accepts the proposal of a wealthy landowner, he will also support her in that?"

Anne shrugged. "I believe he will once his daughter convinces him of her desire for such a match. But, until then, Fitzwilliam may have a hard go of it. I have heard tell he was less than charming when in Hertfordshire, even slighted Miss Bennet, who is her father's favourite."

Richard shook his head in bewilderment at his cousin's ineptitude when it came to Miss Bennet. "Then we shall have to hope the daughter wishes to convince her father of his worth."

"Indeed."

Darcy sauntered into the breakfast room. His cheeks were rosy from the cool morning air, and he wore a most pleased expression on his face as he took his place on Anne's left side and motioned for some tea.

"How is Miss Bennet this morning, Darcy?" Richard teased. If he had expected a glare of displeasure or wall of silence, he was to be disappointed.

The look of pleasure remained firmly in place on Darcy's face. "She is quite well."

"Is she?" He chuckled. "So the struggles of yesterday are over?"

Darcy shook his head. "No, we shall discuss one item of disagreement per walk. As long as I do not add any further injury, all shall be well in a matter of days."

"So you are to meet her each morning?" asked Anne.

Darcy nodded, his smile growing wider.

"And after all is well?" prodded Richard. He heard Anne clear her throat and felt a small kick to his shin but ignored her displeasure. Why was it that women insisted on being so indirect? Surely the more direct approach would garner him the answers he sought and much more quickly than whatever method Anne had in mind.

Darcy looked at Anne with amusement. "I have found it is better to allow him to satisfy his curiosity quickly. He is unbearable until he knows all." He leaned back in his chair and rested his hands on the table, one set of fingers drumming a steady rhythm. "I shall be writing to her father directly for permission to call on her. Then, I must write to Bingley to determine his true feelings regarding Miss Bennet. Then, well, then if all goes well, I will make a trip to Longbourn to speak to her father in regards to marriage." His fingers stopped their drumming and he leaned forward. "Is there any other information you desire?"

Richard laughed. "Not at present, but I reserve the right to question you further in the future."

Darcy shook his head and said as he picked up his cup of tea, "Whether I grant you that right or not, you will still question."

"Indeed," agreed Richard.

Darcy finished his tea and rose to leave. "I shall be in the study should either of you need me," he said and was gone.

Anne raised an eyebrow and tilted her head. "So, my inquisitive cousin, do you suppose he desires to call at the parsonage today?"

Richard rolled his eyes at his neglect to find out that bit of information.

Anne tipped her head toward the door, indicating that Richard should follow their cousin. "I will be in my sitting room. Please, do try to be of use to our cousin. Read his letter before he sends it to her father. And read it as you would should a suitor be seeking Georgiana's attentions. There is no acceptable limit for injury here, Colonel." She smirked at him.

He thought to retort. He even opened his mouth to do so, but instead he gave her a formal bow and said, "Yes, my lady."

~*~*~*~*~*~

So it was that a routine of sorts was established. Darcy would walk in the groves with Elizabeth in the morning while Anne and Richard breakfasted together. Then in the early afternoon, the three cousins would make their way to the parsonage, spending as much time as was allowable without breaching the rules of propriety. It was a routine that Anne found gratifying. She was sure she had never felt so well in all her life, and she credited it to her elevated mood.

On the fourth day of this routine, Anne leaned on Richard's arm as they approached Rosings. She had convinced him that she could walk half the distance from the parsonage, but now she knew he had been correct.

"Are you well?" He asked as he felt her lean into his arm.

"Quite."

"Do you wish a moment to rest?"

"No."

"Are you certain?" Richard slowed his pace. "You are looking quite flushed. Your breathing is laboured, and you are leaning quite heavily on my arm." His pace slowed a bit more. "I would not wish for you to injure yourself just to prove me wrong." He began leading her to a bench that stood near the path.

"It is but a short distance further, Richard. I shall be well."

"Yes, I am sure you will be," he said as he reached the bench and took a seat, "but I desire a rest."

Anne shook her head and joined him on the bench. She was grateful for the rest, but it did rankle that she would have to admit she was not so able as she had supposed. She fixed her eyes on the window of the drawing room, unwilling to meet his eyes, which were watching her carefully. "You were correct," she said softly. "I am still too weak to accomplish such a distance."

"I did not say you were weak. You are not accustomed to the distance." He gave her hand a reassuring pat. "I should have been more insistent and not allowed you to tax yourself to such an extent."

She gave him a wan smile. "I should not have been so resolute."

"We shall lengthen our tour of the garden each day," he said with determination. "You can continue with Mrs. Jenkins when I am gone. And soon you shall be quite strong enough to walk such a distance with ease." He shifted into a more relaxed position. "But for now, you must rest and recover your strength before we continue."

"I do not require a long respite. I shall be able to continue in a moment." He raised an eyebrow at her, and she noted the muscles of his jaw tighten. "Truly, I will be well." She looked back toward the house. "It would do me no good to sit here for too long when my mother is watching. See. She stands there in the drawing room window." She looked at Richard and then back to the house. She sat for a few more minutes before standing and extending her hand to him. "Come, before she summons the doctor or insists upon my taking to my bed."

Richard laughed lightly as he took her hand and tucked it once again into the crook of his arm. He swung his walking stick at the stones on the pathway as they walked. "Does she often watch you from the window? I admit I have never taken the time to notice."

"Only when she has something she wishes to say to me." Anne sighed. "It is usually a complaint. I have been gone too long. I have not worn an appropriately warm cloak. The sun will make me too brown. Her list is quite long and inventive."

They walked silently for several minutes. "I am sorry."

"It is none of your doing. Indeed, it is none of my doing. She has always been overly concerned when it comes to my well-being." She looked at Richard. "It is tiring."

"More than this walk?" Richard teased gently.

"Yes." She smiled. "This walk will be a distant memory before she ever changes her ways."

Richard laughed. "I am sure you are correct. What do you imagine will be the subject of discourse today?"

"Well, you may get scolded for allowing me to be so unladylike as to walk so far. Or she has discovered Darcy is finally seeking his own happiness." They had nearly reached the steps of Rosings. "Whatever it may be, we will know shortly."

Anne handed her wrap and bonnet to a footman as she stepped into the foyer of Rosings.

"Where have you been?" demanded her mother. "I have been waiting for you this past hour, I am sure."

Anne smoothed her skirts and checked her reflection in the mirror. "We called on the parsonage. It is pleasant to have friends at such a close distance."

"Hmph. Friends, indeed." Lady Catherine began walking back to the drawing room. Anne followed, knowing she would hear what her mother had to say whether it was there or in her own sitting room. "They are not of our station. They are acquaintances, nothing more."

Anne rolled her eyes at Richard and shook her head to let him know not to engage her on such a matter.

"Now, Miss Barrows. There is a young lady with whom you should be friends. She could learn much from you, and her status would not damage yours. One must be careful about such things." Lady Catherine seated herself in a purple, tufted chair with a high back and arms that wrapped around and curled out at the top. "Especially now that you insist on subjecting yourself to the rigors of finding a husband." She folded her hands in her lap. "You know, Mr. Barrows is a fine young man. Only a few years older than you. Has a promising future. He is already a well-respected curate with two livings to come to him in the future should he accept them, and why would he not?"

"Mother," interrupted Anne. "Mr. Barrows may be a gentleman, but he is not the gentleman for me."

"But he is from a fine family with a good standing within society. He has no need to travel to London, so your health would not be taxed. I do not understand why you would not even consider such a match."

"I do not like him, and I am certain I could never love him!"

Her mother looked at her and shook her head. "Once, I, too, had the fanciful notion that marriage is about love, but it is not." There was a hint of sorrow in her voice. "It is about securing one's future. Felicity is a happy coincidence should one be so blessed, but it cannot be predicted nor guaranteed."

"I refuse to believe it. You could have been happy with Father if you had chosen to be. He loved you. I saw it in his eyes."

Lady Catherine pressed her lips together in a tight line. Her eyes became hard as she regarded her daughter. Finally, she spoke. "No. It was not love you saw. It was something altogether different."

Anne pressed her. "If it was not love, what was it? He looked at me with the same eyes. Did he not love me?"

"Oh, he loved you as best he could, but he did not love me."

"What was it?" And tried again to get her mother to answer, but she would not.

She turned away from Anne and focused on Richard. "And where is your cousin?"

"He is –" began Richard meaning to explain that Darcy had seen to the curricle while he and Anne walked, but he was interrupted as his absent cousin entered the room.

"Here. I am here," said Darcy. He handed a letter to Richard. "From Georgiana." He nodded to the alcove. Richard stood and went to the window. The seal of the letter had already been broken by Darcy as it was addressed to them both, so it was a simple matter of unfolding the sheets to read. However, he was somewhat startled to find that the first page was not from Georgiana. He raised his eyes to his cousin, who was watching him. Darcy smiled and gave a small nod of his head. Having been given permission, he read the missive from Mr. Bennet.

"How does Georgiana get on?" asked Lady Catherine. "It is a pity she and Anne will not be sisters. They would have gotten on so well together. Georgiana would benefit greatly from having a sister."

Darcy opened his mouth to speak, but Richard was quicker in his reply. "I would not fear, Aunt. I am sure she may have one soon enough." He folded the missive from Mr. Bennet and slid it into his pocket. "Just because Anne does not wish to marry Darcy does not mean no other young lady ever shall."

"Of what is this you speak?" Lady Catherine gave Darcy an appraising look. "Is there another so soon? But, you have only just learned of Anne's refusal." She looked at her daughter and then back to Darcy.

"There was never an offer; there was never an understanding," continued Richard without looking up from the letter he was reading.

"Quite true," agreed Anne. "I imagine there are young ladies with whom Fitzwilliam is acquainted whom he might consider for the position of Mrs. Darcy." She lifted an eyebrow and gave him a small smile.

"He only requires one, Anne." Richard gave his pocket containing the letter a small tap.

Lady Catherine gasped. "What lady would align herself with a gentleman who is known to be attached to another? I am sure such a woman would not be an acceptable sister for Georgiana. Who is she? You must tell me at once!"

"It is no concern of yours." Darcy's posture became rigid, and Anne knew that a battle of wills was about to ensue with her mother demanding and Darcy refusing. She cast an apprehensive eye to Richard, but he was still reading his letter.

"No concern of mine? You throw over my daughter for some trollop? And you say it is no concern of mine?" Lady Catherine's voice rose in volume with each question.

Darcy drew a deep breath. "No one has been thrown over. There was never an engagement."

"Her arts and allurements must be enticing indeed. Is this the sort of woman to whom you wish to expose your sister?"

Darcy pinched the bridge of his nose. A sign, Richard knew, that his cousin was working hard to contain his emotions.

"I assure you, Aunt Catherine, the lady in question is without guile." Darcy's words were clipped. "She would never accept the attentions of a gentleman who was attached. She has far too much integrity for that."

"Then how..." Lady Catherine let her question drop, and her eyes drifted to the window. "She is here."

Chapter 5

Lady Catherine's eyes turned once again toward Darcy. "She is beneath you."

"She is a gentleman's daughter. I am a gentleman's son. We are equals."

Lady Catherine huffed. "Equals indeed! Her father's estate is entailed away. She has relatives in trade. Her portion is small. She seeks your fortune."

Richard stood behind his cousin and gripped his shoulder firmly. He knew that any disparaging comment about someone close to Darcy would provoke his wrath, and he had a feeling a reaction to such comments about Miss Bennet would be worse.

"And you, Aunt? Why did you seek Darcy for Anne when you knew of her father's wishes?" He hoped to turn the conversation away from Miss Bennet.

"We do not speak of my wish to protect and provide for Anne. We speak of the daughter of a gentleman of little standing who wishes to increase her standing by seducing a man of wealth. She is naught but an adventuress — not worthy of your name."

Darcy sprang from his chair. "Not worthy? Not worthy?" The words rattled off the walls and artwork. Lady Catherine shrank back in her chair. Darcy paced the room. His hands clenched and unclenched. He opened his mouth to speak and closed it again. Finally, when he had gained some of his composure, he turned to address his aunt.

"She is no less worthy than Anne. She is, as is my cousin, all that is good and proper." His voice wavered with his barely controlled emotions. "She did not seek me in an attempt to seduce me. It is I who has sought her to court her affections. It is I who must prove myself worthy of her." He turned away, took a step toward the door, but turned again toward his aunt.

"I will brook no disparagement of her person, her character, or her family. You will not interfere with my affairs if you wish to remain connected to me in any way. If I am so fortunate as to win Miss Bennet's hand, you will only be received in our homes if she allows it, so it is to your benefit to seek her good approval. Do I make myself perfectly clear, Madam?"

Lady Catherine gave a small nod of her head.

He looked to Anne. "You shall always be welcome."

His comment seemed to rouse his aunt from her silent state. She turned on her daughter with a vehemence

Richard had not heard from her before. "You knew of this? You encouraged this? I will not have it! You shall not receive that woman in my home, and you shall not call on her. My own daughter! Turned against me by an upstart such as she."

Anne felt the sting of her mother's anger, but it was not unfamiliar to her. She spoke calmly. She knew to match temper for temper may work for her cousin, but he was not Lady Catherine's daughter, nor was he a lady whose words counted for very little. "You may choose not to accept her into our home, but you will not forbid me from calling on the parsonage. The fact that Miss Bennet is currently in residence will not alter my attentions to Mrs. Collins."

"You are my daughter and under my authority. You will do as I say while you are in my home."

Anne had known eventually one day she would have the resolve to go against her mother's wishes and had planned accordingly. She was now only surprised that it had not come to this on the occasion of her refusal to marry Darcy.

"Then, I shall remove myself from your home." She stood and curtseyed to her mother. "You may call on me at the dower house when you have come to your senses. I shall move at first light. I will eat in my room this evening. Good day, Lady Catherine." With her knees shaking and her chin lifted, she managed to make it from the room before she gave way to the emotions such a breach necessarily aroused.

She sank to rest upon the steps of the grand staircase. She knew it was most improper for her to be sitting so with her head in her hands. But she cared not what the servants thought. She knew, as much as she wished to run up those stairs and lock herself away from her mother, her legs would not, simply would not, support her. So here she sat gathering her strength and praying her mother would not find her here.

Thankfully, it was not her mother who found her. Richard sank down on the step beside her and placed his handkerchief on her lap. She peeked up at him and noted Darcy standing near them. She took the handkerchief and dried her eyes.

"You may wish to find another place to rest. She will not remain in that room long," he whispered.

She looked sadly at him and then Darcy. "I do not have the strength at present to conquer the stairs. I fear I am still too shaken. A few moments and I shall be well."

"You do not have time," said Mrs. Jenkins, who had just exited the room, workbasket in hand. "The dragon is already stirring." She winked at Richard, who was shocked to hear the seemingly proper companion use the name that he had used for his aunt for years.

"Colonel Fitzwilliam, if you would be so kind as to carry my charge to her chambers." She did not wait for his response but began ascending the stairs. After a few steps, she looked back at the three who remained at the bottom of the stairs. "We do not have all day if we wish to be settled in our new home by the morrow."

Obediently, Richard hoisted Anne into his arms. She was light; he knew she would be, but it still surprised him as to just how light she was. His surprise deepened as he realized it felt good to have her in his arms. She felt good — soft and vulnerable and precious. His heart stirred with a desire to protect her as she laid her head against his shoulder. Without thought, he kissed her forehead. Startled by his response, he looked first to gauge her reaction. He was relieved when she merely smiled at him and nestled her head into his shoulder a bit more, closing her eyes. Next, he glanced over his shoulder, hoping his cousin had not seen his impulsive act. However, from the look of amusement on Darcy's face, he knew the kiss had not gone unnoticed.

Mrs. Jenkins held open the door to Anne's sitting room. "The chaise by the window, Colonel. It is a most comfortable piece of furniture for reclining. I shall just send for tea, and then we can discuss Miss de Bourgh's removal to the dower house." She slipped out of the room.

Gently, Richard lowered Anne to the chaise. Her eyes remained closed, and she still wore a soft smile on her lips. He placed a pillow behind her head and lifted her feet. Darcy stood to his right, holding out a blanket, his eyes twinkling with delight. Richard took the proffered covering and tucked it gently around Anne, who was now breathing deeply and evenly.

Darcy took a seat while Richard busied himself giving the fire a stir.

"Had I known, I could have stepped aside years ago, Richard." Darcy's tone was light and teasing.

"There is nothing to be known," said Richard taking a seat next to his cousin.

Darcy threw one leg over the other. "You can keep telling yourself that, but trust me, it is much easier to listen to rather than to argue with your heart." His tone was soft and serious.

"I shall keep your advice in mind should I ever require it." Richard shot a sideways look of displeasure at his cousin.

Darcy chuckled. "Yes, nothing to know," he murmured as Mrs. Jenkins entered.

"Oh, my, she has done herself in, has she not?" The lady checked to make sure the blanket was securely tucked around Anne. "A long walk and a disagreement with her mother. Even one twice as strong as Miss de Bourgh would find it exhausting." She moved a book from a small table and motioned for the maid to place the tea tray on it. She moved behind Darcy and tucked the book into place on the shelf. "I do hope the tea will still be warm when she wakes. She usually sleeps for only a few minutes. Too long a rest and it is not restorative but increases the feeling of fatigue." She had returned to the table and was pouring tea for the gentlemen. Richard thought how her busy actions and chatter reminded him of a hummingbird flitting about. He had never seen her do more than occupy a corner before.

But seeing her now, he understood why Anne enjoyed her company so much.

Having served tea to both the gentlemen, she sat down, balancing her cup and saucer on her lap. "We really do not have time to wait for Miss de Bourgh to wake. Plans must be put into action." She lifted her cup and took a small sip of tea.

"Plans into action?" questioned Darcy. "She has plans made for a situation like this?"

"One does not live with a mother such as Lady Catherine without making plans for an eventual confrontation," reasoned Mrs. Jenkins. "Although we had expected it to happen sooner than this." She gave Darcy a pointed look.

"But, no matter the timing, things must be set in motion. First, I have maids already attending to the packing of Miss de Bourgh's things. Mrs. Kellet will supervise the detailed cleaning of Miss de Bourgh's suite of rooms, which will be the reason given to all as to why Miss de Bourgh has left her home. It simply would not be good for her health with her fragile constitution to be exposed to the dust of such a cleaning. Then, there are the plans for a small house party to celebrate her birthday. The dower house will be the perfect spot for such an intimate gathering, especially with the cleaning taking place here." She sipped her tea again.

"And staffing?" Richard asked. "How do we provide staffing?"

"Mr. Kellet will notify the necessary people. There is no need to fear a lack of staffing. You will find Miss de Bourgh has a wealth of loyal servants." Mrs. Jenkins paused and looked seriously at the gentleman seated near her. She lowered her voice. "She does not, however, have a large number of friends to invite to a party. Those she does have are of her mother's choosing, if you take my meaning. So, we will require your assistance with creating a list of people to invite." She set her cup aside and rose to retrieve writing supplies.

"You will both attend, of course. And Lady Matlock knows she will be called on to act as chaperone. Miss de Bourgh does not wish for many to attend. Three or four ladies and an equal number of gentlemen, I suppose." She wrote down the names as she mentioned them. Then she looked expectantly at the gentlemen.

"Georgiana, of course," said Richard. "And Darcy, do you think you could persuade Bingley to attend without his sisters?"

"Bingley will not say no to a party." Darcy drummed his fingers on the arm of his chair. "I am wondering if we ought to invite Miss Bennet — Miss Jane Bennet that is. She is currently visiting relatives in London. I am sure Miss Elizabeth would be delighted to see her. She has mentioned wishing to see her sister. However, I am not sure if Miss Bennet would appreciate Bingley's presence."

Richard smirked at Darcy's look of unease. "A further discussion for the groves tomorrow morning?"

Darcy's features relaxed. "Of course, I shall ask her tomorrow. We can remove Bingley's name from the list, if necessary."

"Oh, of course," said Mrs. Jenkins as she scribbled down two more names below Mr. Bingley's. "Miss Elizabeth and Miss Maria. They must attend." She tapped her chin. "We are still short on eligible gentlemen."

"Darcy, what of Mr. Pruett? He was in town when we left."

Darcy nodded. "Not too old, second son, no substantial inheritance. A plausible choice."

Richard felt the significance of why his cousin listed the man's qualifications. "I am sure Colonel Alcock would attend, but the wife of an officer does not seem the right role for Anne."

"We could invite him just the same," said Mrs. Jenkins. "A man need not keep his commission if he marries an heiress, after all."

Richard heard a small chuckle from his cousin.

"That is a nice group. I believe Miss Maria and Miss

Darcy are about the same age and will find companionship. Four gentlemen and three ladies, so nearly equal numbers." She wore a satisfied smile. "Well, best get to it, then, gentlemen. There are several letters that require writing and must be sent express. Time is of the essence."

Richard and Darcy rose to go do as they had been bid.

"Your mother will arrive today, Richard," Anne commented sleepily from the chaise.

Richard's brow furrowed. "Today?"

"Mmm hmm." Anne stretched and sat up. "I wrote to her of my plans to refuse Darcy, and she insisted on arriving a week before my birthday. She expected my mother to be difficult."

"Does Aunt Catherine know of this?"

"No, your mother insisted on arriving unannounced. I think she enjoys tormenting mother since mother insists on insulting your father on a regular basis." Anne smiled. "Presently, I do not mind her penchant to annoy my mother."

Richard was pleased that Anne looked refreshed. When she had fallen asleep so quickly in his arms, he had worried she might be unwell. "I will be on hand to greet her and inform her of what is afoot."

Anne smiled. "Just as I wished. Thank you."

Richard paused. "You are well?"

"I am well. I just tire easily. You will...both...return to visit me this evening?"

"You know my mother will insist on it," said Richard.

Darcy also acknowledged his desire to spend the evening in her company rather than that of Lady Catherine. When he was outside the door, he clapped Richard on the shoulder and murmured, "Easier to listen." Then with a chuckle, he strode down the hall to his room.

Richard stood for a moment in the hall. He could not shrug off the feeling that some great shift had occurred for him this afternoon, but certainly it was not as his love-struck cousin suggested. Was it? No, certainly it was not. He walked determinedly to his room to write his letter of invitation, though, he hoped Colonel Alcock would not be able to attend.

Chapter 6

Winnifred Fitzwilliam, Lady Matlock, alighted from her carriage and straightened her pelisse before taking the proffered arm of her son. Richard told her briefly of what had transpired that afternoon.

"Some women should not be mothers," she muttered. Richard smiled at the determination he could see on her face. She turned to her abigail and instructed that only what was necessary for tonight and tomorrow morning be taken to her rooms. The rest of her belongings should be stored and ready for transport to the dower house at first light.

"Well, then, shall we, my son?" She asked. "Take me to my niece."

"You do not wish to greet Aunt Catherine first?" he asked.

She sighed in exasperation. "If you think we must, but I do believe she will be more put out if I greet her daughter first."

Richard chuckled. "Then allow me to escort you to your niece."

Mr. Kellet opened the door to Rosings and bowed low. "My lady, this is an unexpected surprise." A small smile played at his mouth. He lowered his voice. "Mrs. Kellet has had your room prepared both here and at the dower house. I can have your things delivered there directly?"

"Whatever you deem best, Mr. Kellet. I will trust your judgement to arrange matters."

"Yes, my lady." He bowed once again. "Do you wish to be announced, my lady?"

"No, thank you, Mr. Kellet. I shall attend Miss de Bourgh first. I do apologize for the disturbance my arrival will cause."

His eyes twinkled with amusement. "'Tis no hardship, my lady." With one last bow, he left to make arrangements for Lady Matlock's things to be taken to the dower house.

"He must have the patience of Job to put up with her as his employer," she whispered to Richard. "The next master of Rosings will have a treasure in that man should he have the sense to retain Mr. Kellet. Your father tried to hire him away from Catherine, but he would hear none of it. Said he promised his master to look after the ladies of Rosings, and he is not a man to go back on his word. He keeps a close eye on things. If you ever need information on any who visit here, he is the person to see."

Richard's eyes grew wide at this information. "Indeed?"

She laughed softly. "How do you suppose I always knew what you and Darcy were up to when you were young?"

He shook his head. "I should have known you had a spy working for you." He opened the door to Anne's sitting room and allowed his mother to enter before him. Before she even spoke a word of greeting, she gathered Anne into her arms.

"How are you, my darling? Richard has told me you have had a trying day."

Anne felt the tears well up in her eyes. How she longed for such motherly compassion on a regular basis. "I am well, Aunt Winnie."

"And my son and his cousin? Are they caring for you?"

Anne smiled at Richard. "They are. Richard more than Fitzwilliam."

"Indeed?" Lady Matlock raised her brows and gave Richard an assessing look. "Darcy is falling behind my son in seeing to duty? What has the world come to?"

"Darcy is doing his duty, Mother. But his attentions are divided at present."

He saw the curiosity in his mother's eyes. "So this Miss Bennet has finally snared the elusive Mr. Darcy, has she?"

Anne laughed. "It is more a matter of our besotted cousin snaring the lovely Miss Bennet."

"Besotted? Oh, this I must see!" She giggled at the thought. "And he has had to work for it? I imagine he never expected with his money and connections to have to do such a thing. I cannot wait to meet her."

"He has not won her hand yet," cautioned Richard.

"Ah, but he will," said Lady Matlock. "I understand your mother has some objections to her? And this has led to your removal to the dower house tomorrow morning?"

Anne nodded. "I expected she would be trying once she knew of my decision to not marry her choice, but to have him happily attached to another was more than she could pretend to abide." Anne sighed. "Miss Bennet has been a friend to me these last three weeks. She accepts me for who I am. She makes no claim on me other than friendship of the truest kind. As Fitzwilliam said, she is without guile. She possesses great intelligence and wit. She is everything that would complement my cousin. That she loves him as completely as he obviously loves her makes it all the sweeter."

"If she is all that, what objections does your mother have other than the obvious that she is not you?"

"She is a gentleman's daughter, but the gentleman is of little standing. She is the second of five daughters, and her dowry is minimal. Her mother has one brother who is a solicitor and another who is in trade. Mother claims that she is beneath Fitzwilliam and not worthy of the Darcy name."

Lady Matlock gasped, her hand flying to her chest. She looked first to Anne and then Richard. "She did not say that to Darcy?"

"She most certainly did."

"Oh, dear. Is he still in residence?"

Anne nodded. "He spoke very directly to my mother about what he expects of her in the future if she wishes to keep a family tie to him."

"He did? Darcy threatened a breach in the family?"

"You would have been impressed, Mother. After his initial outburst, which rattled the windows, he was very forthcoming with his thoughts."

"Darcy raised his voice?"

"He did." Anne grasped her aunt's arm. "His defence of her was quite romantic, Aunt Winnie. He even told Mother if he were to be fortunate enough to secure Miss Bennet, it would be Miss Bennet who would decide if she would ever be accepted into any of his homes, so it was in her best interest to treat Miss Bennet with kindness."

Richard rolled his eyes as both women sighed.

"Then, he told me I would always be welcome, and that is when mother figured out I had played a role in bringing Fitzwilliam and Miss Bennet together. That is when she told me I was forbidden to continue my friendship with the lady. Oh, those are not the exact words she used, but it was her meaning."

"And that," said Richard with respect colouring his

voice, "is when Anne took her stand and why Anne, Darcy and I will be moving in the morning."

"And tell me of the plans for the move. I know there is a party to be planned."

Richard took this as his cue to leave. He had done his part in writing his invitation. He was quite happy to leave the remaining details to the ladies. "I shall inform Darcy of your arrival. He should be back from his ride now."

Lady Matlock smiled and waved him off, but not without noting how his gaze lingered just a little longer on Anne and the smiles that were exchanged.

~*~*~*~*~*~

Richard knocked his normal pattern on Darcy's door, waited for a count of ten, and then entered. "Mother is here. She is visiting with Anne. She has not yet greeted our aunt."

Darcy looked up from the book he was reading.

"Did you not go riding?"

"I did. Stopped in the village for a pint with old man Coburg. It's tradition, you know."

Richard nodded. "How is the old chap doing? Still running the place or has he finally given it over to his son?"

"His son is in charge, mostly. You know he will not give up control before he ceases to breathe."

"You do not smell like horse, so I assume you have been back for some time. Why did you not come to Anne's room? Surely you saw the coach and knew Mother was here?"

Darcy looked at the wall behind Richard and worried his lip with his teeth.

"Out with it, Darcy. You do not need to smooth over whatever it is for my sake. I can handle whatever horrid news you have to share."

"Who says I am about to impart something unpleasant?"

"You are biting your lip and looking past me. You always do that when you are unsure how someone is going to react to whatever it is you have to say. So out with it."

Richard drew a chair closer to where Darcy sat and made himself comfortable.

"I overheard a conversation in the pub. You know how the backs of the benches are so high that you cannot see over them?"

"Makes it a nice cozy spot for discussions." Richard winked at Darcy.

They had always teased each other about kissing the barmaids behind the benches though neither had.

"Yes, well, there were none of those sorts of discussions taking place."

"Never are in Coburg's."

"But the conversation I heard has left me feeling uneasy. I am not quite sure what to do about it."

"Did you see who was talking?"

Darcy nodded. "Barrows and another man he called Clarke."

Richard felt a sense of dread settling in his stomach.

"It seems someone has told Barrows of Anne's financial situation. He seems quite interested."

"Exactly what did he say?" Richard sat near the edge of his chair and leaned toward his cousin.

Darcy shifted uneasily. "Remember I am only repeating what was said."

Richard nodded and attempted to assume a more relaxed posture.

"Barrows was sitting behind me. Coburg had gone to help his son with something. There were only a few patrons in the place, and none was near where I sat. Barrows says…"

"Did you hear Rosings was left to de Bourgh's daughter? But only if she doesn't marry that prig Darcy?" Barrows sat his mug on the table with a definite thud.

"No, thought it was entailed away or some such nonsense. Never heard specifics."

"None was given. A shadowy business it was. Seems the daughter just found out and finally called off her engagement to Darcy. So, this is my chance to acquire an estate with very little effort."

"The other man, Clarke, laughed rather loudly and called for two more pints. They did not continue talking until the barmaid had delivered their ale. Then Clarke says to Barrows...."

"I wouldn't call getting leg shackled very little effort. Perhaps you can worm your way into a marriage, but marriage is not for the short duration. I would not be tied to that harridan of de Bourgh's for an estate twice Rosings. And you have to get her to accept you."

"She'll accept me. Her mother is already promoting me, what with her and my own mother being friends and all. And, I also have some information that neither mother or daughter would wish to be spread far and wide."

"So you force their hand. You're now stuck not only with two women in your care, but two angry women. Like I said, marriage is not for the short duration."

"Yes, it is 'til death do us part." There was a moment of extended silence.

"What are you playing at, Barrows?"

"She's frail. It is unlikely she will survive childbirth. Her mother, of course, will be overwrought with grief. It is a simple matter of having her committed to Bedlam or hiring the finest actor of questionable standards to medicate her into an early grave. Thus, the estate should be free and clear of all entanglements within a year."

"That is all I heard as a group of men came in and took a table near us. Barrows and Clarke left shortly after. I waited another quarter hour before exiting so they would not know I had been there." Darcy rose and walked to the window, turning his back to Richard to allow for some privacy as he processed all that he had just heard. "You know she will not accept him without coercion. We need to discover what secret he knows."

"He would kill her for an estate?" Richard still sat in his chair staring at where Darcy had been. He shook his head to clear the fog from it. "I expected we would need to protect her from fortune hunters, but I never expected them to be murderous in their intent."

He rose and paced the length of the room. His heart could not or would not stop pounding within his chest. He felt as though the contents of his stomach might, at any moment, choose to be no longer confined within him. He had not felt this unsettled since his first foray into battle. His desire to relieve a man of his life had never been so strong. But this was not a battle where he could run the enemy through with his sword; no, they must think of tactics and plans. They had the advantage of their enemy being unaware of their knowledge of his plans, however. Finally, the room stopped its spinning, and he was able to begin to think.

"You are right, of course, Darcy. If we knew what information he holds, we might be able to limit his ability to force Anne into an acceptance of his suit." He pulled at his neckcloth. The room was standing still, but it was so unreasonably warm.

"He could not present a suit at all if she were to marry

before he has time to put his plan into action," suggested Darcy.

Richard stopped his pacing to concentrate his efforts on that bothersome cravat. "But whom would she marry? She has no suitors. There are the men we invited to the house party, but it does not give her a very large selection from which to choose. I will not force her to make an uninformed choice. She deserves better than a rushed marriage to a man she barely knows. What if he does not love her? What if she does not love him? She would be condemned to a life of misery. I cannot be part of that." The offensive piece of cloth finally found its way to the chair, but now it seemed his jacket had suddenly become uncomfortably snug.

"And what if there is one there whom she loves, and he loves her?" Darcy tried not to look at his cousin. This discussion was of a serious nature, but Richard's tugging at his clothing was humorous. His cousin would not appreciate a smile or a laugh at this particular moment.

"Do you really think one of the men in attendance will suit?" Richard's coat had joined his cravat on the chair, and he had begun working at the fastenings of his waistcoat.

"Indeed I do, but we should still try to discover the information of which Barrows speaks."

Richard's hands stopped. "Kellet."

"What?"

"We must speak to Mr. Kellet. If anyone around here — other than our aunt, who I assume will not speak to us of secrets — knows anything, it will be Mr. Kellet." Richard turned to exit the room.

Darcy cleared his throat and held out Richard's jacket and neckcloth.

"You may get further if you are attired appropriately, Cousin."

Richard smiled sheepishly and after tying his cravat, allowed Darcy to assist him with his coat.

Darcy smoothed his hands across the tops of Richard's shoulders and gave each seam a slight tug, removing any remaining creases. "Truthfully, it is much easier to listen."

"Listen?" Richard looked at his cousin in confusion. Of course, he planned to listen to what Mr. Kellet had to say.

Darcy shook his head. "Your heart, Richard. You. Love. Anne. And not as a cousin." He opened the door and motioned for his dazed cousin to exit ahead of him.

Chapter 7

Lady Matlock waited until she saw Lady Catherine reach for her glass at the end of dinner before broaching a topic which she knew would not be well-received.

"Catherine." She paused. Lady Catherine looked at her expectantly, her wine glass halted in its progress to her lips. "No, please, have some wine before I continue. You may find you need it."

Lady Catherine's brow furrowed, but she sipped her wine and blotted her mouth with her napkin.

"Since Mrs. Kellet is having Anne's rooms thoroughly cleaned, I was wondering if this might not be the best time to have them redecorated for you." Lady Matlock paused a moment, but not so long that her sister-in-law had time to speak. "Since Anne is soon to marry, it would be best to have her return to the mistress' suite. I expect her husband will be taking the master's suite of rooms. It would be dashed awkward to have his room adjoining yours, do you not think? It would not be at all proper to have him traipsing about the house in search of his wife."

Lady Catherine's mouth hung open, and it took a moment for her to collect herself before she could reply. Plates were removed, glasses refilled. "Married soon?" She rose and gave Darcy a pointed look. "I do not see how that is to happen when she has no suitors." She proceeded to move to the sitting room, wine glass in hand.

"Oh, but she is a beautiful young woman in possession of a large fortune. She shall not be in want of a husband for long," reasoned Lady Matlock. "Why I know of several young men of my acquaintance who would suit. I only need an opportunity to make the introductions." Lady Matlock seated herself near Lady Catherine while Darcy and Richard placed themselves at a chess game nearby.

"But not in London," interjected Darcy. "Anne wishes to marry from Kent."

Lady Matlock pondered this information. "That will make it a trifle more difficult, but not impossible."

"I will not have her marrying anyone associated with James. I will not trust them, for I do not trust him."

"I really do not understand why you are so set against your own brother, Catherine. Whatever did he do to lose your faith in him? As he tells it, you were very close when you were children."

Richard watched a shadow of sadness pass across his aunt's face before her features once again grew hard.

"That was long ago and many things have happened between then and now, some can never be undone, so it does not signify." She looked sternly at Darcy and Richard. "I trust you both know a young lady is more than a mere pawn to be used and sacrificed in the play of a game?" She had risen and stood beside the game table. Purposefully, she moved a few pieces on the board. "I am trusting you — as I have been left no other option — to protect my daughter as if she were the most valuable piece on that board — no matter the cost."

Richard studied the scene she had left. His king, the most valuable piece, stood in danger with merely a pawn for protection. He had two options; one offered him a move closer to capturing Darcy's king while the other would allow him to protect his pawn and subsequently his king. If he took the first option, his pawn would surely be taken and his king would be more difficult, though not impossible, to defend. Should he choose the second option, he would strengthen the defense around his king, but his queen, his most powerful piece of defense, would be lost.

He knew his skills as a player; to lose the pawn and place Darcy's king closer to capture was the route he would have decided upon in normal play, but this was not normal play. He was to imagine that pawn as Anne and defend her as he would his king. Without a second thought, he left his queen to be captured.

Richard looked at the hand which lay on his shoulder and then to the face of his aunt. She smiled softly at him.

It was a new expression. For a moment, a mere moment, he glimpsed the vulnerability within her. To say that this startled him would be owning only half the truth. He had never thought of her as anything but the epitome of strength and determination. So strong, so determined, that, at times, she was very like a dragon, hunting and slaying as it saw fit, ruling its domain with tenacity.

Richard's eyes returned to the board as he watched Darcy capture his queen. He wondered if fear provoked her tenacity. He had seen battle. Even the most soft-spoken of soldiers became as a roaring lion in the face of peril. What had his aunt faced that had caused her to become as she now was? He hoped his conversation with Mr. Kellet, whom he had yet to question, would be enlightening.

As chance would have it, the very gentleman entered the room carrying a letter on a tray. "Begging your pardon, sir. It seems this was not delivered to you as it should have been." He bowed and extended the tray to Richard. Richard took the letter and thanked the butler. He turned the letter over in his hand, his brows pulled together.

Darcy gave him a quizzical look.

"It is from Alcock."

"A reply?" asked Darcy softly so that others in the room might not hear.

"Impossible. It is not an express. This was marked yesterday."

"Billiards?" Darcy offered rising to leave the room.

Richard nodded and followed. He broke the seal as he walked and as soon as they had entered the room, he dropped into a chair and began reading the contents. Darcy patiently arranged the balls on the table and then leaned against its edge, cue in hand, arms folded across his chest, one foot crossed over the other.

Richard drew in and then expelled a large breath. "There are more rumblings of war from America."

Darcy nodded. "That is not new. There has been unrest for some time in that quarter, what with the trade restrictions and all."

Richard shook his head. "The unrest is deepening. Gore has returned from the Canadas, and there are mutterings of Brock needing reinforcements against a possible attack on British North American holdings."

"Brock? He would be hoping for experienced men, would he not?"

Richard nodded and took up his cue. "To protect against desertions."

Darcy took his shot. "And you are experienced." He watched his ball roll across the table, hitting just where he had hoped. "There is talk that your company will be called to go."

Richard laid his cue on the table and ran his hands through his hair. He could not concentrate on a game. "Save for a few, the whole company has experience. It would be an ideal unit to send."

"How soon?"

"Alcock expects the decision will be made known within the month. I could be gone before summer." He had returned to his chair, his head rested on the back of it, his hands scrubbed at his face. "It would not be a short tour. A year, minimum, but there is no guarantee that things will conclude so quickly. Look at France. How many coalitions have there been, and the Corsican still tramples where he wills?"

Darcy took a seat near his cousin and waited. He knew Richard would eventually speak about what truly troubled him concerning this news.

"I knew when I purchased my first commission I could and would be called on to serve his majesty in locations far from home. And I have served on foreign soil for long stretches of time in desperate conditions, but..." His voice trailed off. He lifted his hands and shrugged. How could he admit to no longer wishing to serve?

"You have served well. Was not your unit distinguished for its excellent service? To step aside and allow another to take your place would not be unthinkable. You have spoken of doing so before."

"But what do I step aside to do? This is what I was trained to be. I am a second son, I must earn my way."

Darcy rested his steepled fingers against his chin. "Or, you must marry well."

"I have no time to find an heiress before I make this

decision, Darcy. If the decision is to be made in a month's time, I must sell my commission before it has been made public so that I do not look like a deserter. I could not bear to bring such shame to my family. And what family would wish to tie themselves to a disloyal second son with little income?"

"Deserter?" Darcy was incredulous. "A deserter is one who runs from his duty, leaving his fellow soldiers at a disadvantage. I know you would not leave your men unless you knew they were in capable hands. Did you not mention a Wetherald who has been hoping to purchase a higher commission?"

Richard stared at his cousin. "You are right. Wetherald has been anxious to move up, and he is an excellent soldier, good seat, excellent with both firearm and sword. But last I heard he was still saving his tuppence. He may not be able to purchase my commission from me."

"Would he be adverse to a loan?"

"Darcy! I cannot have you buying my commission."

"Why? I am free to do as I see fit with my income and using it to assure the continued safety of my sister's guardian seems a good use. Besides, I am not buying your commission, I am aiding one of his majesty's finest to advance in the ranks. A repayment schedule will be drawn up. It will be a business arrangement, nothing more, nothing less."

Richard raised his brows in disbelief.

Darcy smiled sheepishly. "Very well. It will be a business arrangement where I do not care if I lose money as the safety of my money is not the main objective." He rose and straightened his coat. "So it is settled. You will introduce me to Wetherald. I will make him my offer of support, and your commission shall be yours no longer. You are welcome to stay with me until such time as you find an heiress to marry."

There was a light rap at the door before it began to push open. "Might we join you?" Richard's mother poked her head inside the door. "Anne was getting lonely up in her rooms, so we came in search of company."

She opened the door the rest of the way and allowed Anne to enter before her.

"Oh, please, stay seated," said Anne as Richard made an attempt to rise at her entrance. She took the cue Richard had discarded on the table earlier. "I wish to play."

"You play?" questioned Richard. She definitely held the cue as if she was experienced.

"Mr. Kellet taught Mrs. Jenkins and me. It can become quite dull around here at times."

Darcy laughed. "And your mother allows this?"

Anne's eyes sparkled. "I have convinced her it is an appropriate amount of exercise for one with my constitution." She eyed the table. "I assume it is my turn since Darcy is not stalking his prey."

"Stalking my prey?"

"Yes, you become decidedly focused when there is a plan to make. Your eyes narrow, you pace, the room could catch fire about you, but you would continue with your ruminations until the plan was formed to perfection. Very like an animal intent on capturing its next meal. So since you are standing there conversing, I assume it is not yet your turn to eliminate your opponent?"

Darcy scowled. "Take your turn."

Anne laughed and did just that.

Darcy eyed where the balls lay on the table. "I think I should know if the room was on fire," he muttered.

Lady Matlock smoothed Richard's hair back into place. "The news was not good?" she asked.

Richard shook his head.

"Will you tell me? Or will you think it will worry me too greatly?" She took the chair next to Richard where Darcy had been sitting and eyed the letter that lay folded on the table between them. "From Colonel Alcock?"

Richard nodded.

"So it is as your father feared. You are to go to Canada."

"Canada?" Anne's cue connected with her ball at an odd angle. Her gaze being drawn first to her aunt and then Richard.

"There has been no announcement," said Richard. "It is merely conjecture."

"But Canada?" said Anne again.

"There is talk of reinforcing the border against possible invasion by the Americans," explained Lady Matlock. "It is all very vexing to be sure. Matlock has been talking of the unrest for weeks now."

"There is naught to fear, Aunt," said Darcy. "Richard is to sell his commission. He will remain in England."

"You will sell your commission?" Richard was sure he heard a faint amount of hope in her voice. She had never been comfortable with his choice of profession.

"I am considering it."

"But it must be done quickly, mustn't it?" He was certain he could now hear the excitement in her voice.

"If I sell it, I will no longer have an occupation. Darcy has offered to let me stay with him for a time, but I must re-establish myself in some useful manner. A source of income must be found." He looked at Darcy, hoping that his cousin would not mention the part about marriage.

"An estate. You need an estate." His mother's enthusiasm was growing.

"And how do you expect me to get an estate, mother. I do not have that kind of blunt."

"But your father has connections. I am sure there is someone who would be willing to negotiate a reasonable agreement. And, you are the second son of the Earl of Matlock. There are many who would desire the family connection. You are an attractive young gentleman, I have no doubt you could marry some heiress."

"Mother," he groaned. "You are partial to me because I am your son. I assure you, I am not the catch you think I am."

Anne had come to sit across from Richard and his mother. She had been listening intently to all they had been saying. "No, no, she is right." Her heart raced as she considered what she was about to say. "You need an estate. Your skills would be well used in its running. You can manage people, and you can foresee problems. Added to that, you have a compassionate heart that would surely garner loyalty from your servants and tenants."

She dared to look up from her hands, which were clasped tightly in her lap, to see what his reaction was to her words. What she saw made her falter for a moment. His shock was evident in the slight opening of his mouth and the wideness of his eyes. But his eyes were also filled with what looked like pleasure at her words of praise. Perhaps her idea would not meet with immediate rejection. Perhaps there was hope. Her heart dearly wished it to be so. She took a breath and allowed her eyes to dart first to her aunt's smiling face before returning to study her hands.

"You are as handsome as you are good." She blushed. "Any young woman would be deliriously happy to marry such a gentleman, but you must not marry just any heiress." She swallowed. "You must marry me."

She heard the gasps from her cousins and aunt and

hurried on lest one of them should stop her from speaking. "As you know, I have an estate and a substantial dowry, both are things you need. But that is not why you must marry me." Anne bit her lip and twisted her hands. "Oh, I do not know if I can say it."

He took her hands in his. "Look at me." His voice was soft. She lifted her eyes to his face, his face that wore a hopeful smile. "Do you...could you...eventually...do you think you might come to love me?" He stammered.

She shook her head ever so slightly, and his eyes began to lose their light, his smile began to fade. She shrugged. "I already do. That is why you must marry me, for I could not bear to see you married to another."

"You love me?" The door closed softly behind Lady Matlock and Darcy. "How? When? Why?" His mind was filled with questions. He did not understand how he could have been so fortunate to have earned her love. He still wondered at his own love for her. If she were to ask him these same questions, he was not sure he would be able to answer them.

"I truly do not know." Anne laughed lightly. "I know I have loved you all my life, but it was not until...well...I am not sure where it changed from the love one has for a cousin to the love one has for a man." She looked at him in confusion, her cheeks rosy.

"But the knowledge of it has been a slow realization which started while I anxiously awaited you to be with me when I was to confront my mother with that letter." She clasped his hands more tightly. "There was none I desired to be at my side more than you. And when you would greet me each morning with a kiss." She rubbed her thumb lightly across his knuckles as she spoke. "I longed for it to be so each day. And when I was tired and you forced me to rest, and then you carried me to my room when I lacked the strength to take the stairs on my own, I knew I wished to always be cared for in such a way." The words tumbled from her mouth, one thought falling on top of another.

"When you mentioned you may be sent to Canada," she looked at him earnestly, "I thought my heart had been rent from my chest. I cannot describe the relief I felt when Darcy let it be known you were to sell your commission." Her gaze softened, and she smiled. "As your mother spoke of making a favourable match, I knew what I had to do." She lifted his hands to her lips and kissed them. "I must offer for you." She slid from her chair and knelt before him. "Will you accept me? Will you allow me to be your wife?"

He withdrew his hands from hers, so he might use them to cup her lovely face. "My Anne." His voice was filled with admiration. "My beautiful, beautiful Anne." He leaned forward and brushed his lips across hers before pulling back slightly and looking into her eyes. "Nothing, absolutely nothing, would make me happier than to call you my wife." He kissed her lightly once more before taking her hands and helping her to her feet, so he could draw her into his embrace and kiss her more thoroughly.

Chapter 8

Darcy leaned against the wall in the hall outside the billiard's room. He looked at his watch. "How long do you suppose we should wait?"

"Five more minutes should do." Lady Matlock sat on a small bench across from him.

"Do we tell Lady Catherine?"

Lady Matlock shook her head. "As things stand between Anne and her mother, it really must be her decision."

Darcy nodded.

"You will approve of her suitor, will you not?" Lady Matlock smirked and raised an eyebrow. "I am sure you will get no opposition from Richard." She covered her mouth with her hand to contain a laugh.

Darcy smiled. "I am quite certain that Richard will only accept one answer."

"Indeed." Lady Matlock smoothed an invisible wrinkle from her skirt. "You did not come to see Anne this afternoon."

"I chose to read after my ride."

"Ah. I see." Her tone of voice told him she did not believe his reason. She folded her arms, tapped a finger on her arm, and looked at him expectantly.

He shook his head and pinched the bridge of his nose. "Very well. I needed some time to think."

"Did something happen at Cobergs?"

Darcy's brows rose in surprise. "How — no, do not tell me. Kellet?"

Lady Matlock tapped her nose with her finger.

"Does the man know everything?" Darcy asked incredulously.

"He is very resourceful."

Darcy pulled his watch from his pocket once again. "Would he know anything about a secret my aunt does not wish to be made known?" He asked casually as he checked the time.

"Why do you ask? Has something been said?" There was a hint of something unsettled in her voice though Darcy could not put a name to it.

"Did Kellet not tell you?" He smiled when he heard the huff of exasperation the question was meant to evoke. He lowered his voice. "Not much has been said, yet it is enough to raise concern." He pushed off from the wall. "Our time is up. Shall we interrupt?" He rapped on the door before pushing it open.

"Are we to wish you happy?" Darcy bit back a smile at

the spectacle before him. Richard's cravat was askew; his hair was rumpled while Anne's cheeks glowed a rosy red, and at least one hairpin had worked its way loose.

A smile split Richard's face. "Whether you wish it or not, we are happy."

"Yes, about that." Darcy began to pour a set of celebratory drinks. "Is there not someone who needs to grant permission before you can assume your happiness?" He lifted a teasing eyebrow at Anne.

She narrowed her eyes and crossed her arms. "I believe I have the approbation of one of my advisors."

"It certainly appears you do," murmured Darcy, earning a glare from Anne. He handed her a small glass of wine. "And your other advisor, do you expect it will be a challenge to earn his approval?" He handed a glass of wine to his aunt, who was clearly enjoying the teasing.

"Well," said Anne as she took a seat near the fire. "At one time, he was the most serious and thoughtful fellow, but I fear he has changed recently. There seems to be something about him that is different, a lightness to his air, a lack of worry that is most disturbing. I do hope this change has not addled his thinking so much that he cannot see the wisdom in such a match as Richard."

Darcy chuckled as he joined the group near the fire. "I would fear for his mental capabilities if he were unable to see the benefit to both of you." He sipped his drink. "But, I understand he has come to learn recently that there is more to marriage than advantageous alignments. Thanks to the help of some very astute friends and cousins..." He dipped his head in a small bow of gratitude "...your other advisor finds himself on the brink of such happiness as you currently claim and would most assuredly give his blessing."

He sat his drink aside and donned his business façade. "Of course, the details of the marriage must be worked out thoroughly so that all parties are satisfied, and the future of Anne and any issue from the union would be secured as stipulated by Uncle Louis' documents. However, even before we get to such details as those, there is the issue of the selling of Richard's commission. A letter must be written and sent as soon as possible on that account."

"I shall write it before I retire tonight. Will you include your offer?"

Darcy nodded. "I think it most expedient if both the notice of selling and the offer of assistance be made simultaneously."

Lady Matlock gave her son a questioning look.

"I know of a man in my unit who is looking to move up in rank. He is well-suited for my position, and I would feel a great deal of peace leaving my men in his care. I do not know whether he has the blunt to purchase the commission."

His mother nodded her understanding. "And Darcy

has offered to extend the man some credit — money he realizes may not be regained?"

"Money he will not ask to be returned," said Darcy. "I shall supplement whatever he lacks for the purchase as a gift."

"A gift?" Anne asked.

"I consider it an investment in the happiness of two most beloved cousins." His cheeks pinked a bit at such an admission. "What is wealth if it cannot be used in creating happiness and security for those we love? I shall hear no objections regarding my decision."

Lady Matlock reached over and patted her nephew's arm. "Your mother would be proud. She used to say those very words. I believe she drove her father to distraction at times with her insistence on giving where she saw a need. Thankfully, she married a man who encouraged that trait in both her and her children."

"Thank you, Aunt." Darcy took another sip of his drink before returning it to the table and his attention to the matters at hand. "Anne, your mother will need to be made aware of your betrothal, but how and when you wish to inform her is entirely up to you. My hope is that, by the end of your house party, she will have come to her senses regarding Miss Bennet and all will be restored to some semblance of normal."

"An announcement of your engagement may help her

come to her senses more quickly," suggested Lady Matlock.

"Indeed it would," agreed Anne. "But I prefer that she come to her senses without such aid."

"As do I," agreed Darcy.

"There are reasons for her determination," said Richard. "I do not know what they are, but not even our aunt does not act without cause. There is a reason she insisted on Darcy as a husband for Anne. There is also a reason she will not allow Anne to go to London." He held up a hand to forestall the comments he knew he would face from both Anne and his mother. "A reason other than her health. And then there is the secret you heard mentioned, Darcy. After her demonstration at the chess table, I cannot help but think that the reasons all lead to the protection of Anne, though, I cannot begin to imagine how they tie together."

Anne looked between Darcy and Richard. "And what secret is this?"

Both men shrugged. "That is just it. We have no idea what it is, but we do have reason to believe that someone is planning to use it to their advantage to force Anne into accepting his offer." Darcy turned to his aunt. "That is what I was contemplating this afternoon following my ride."

Richard looked at his mother. She appeared a bit pale and startled, but she did not look so curious as he knew she could be. There was no narrowing of her eyes or lift of a brow nor was there any pursing of her lips. "We may not need to talk to Kellet, Darcy. I believe I know someone who will be a far better source of information." He smiled as his mother's eyes grew wide, and she gave her head the slightest of shakes. "Oh, no, Mother. You must tell us what you know if we plan to protect your future daughter."

"Perhaps, Richard," said Anne. "You should explain exactly how I am in danger. Surely whoever this gentleman is who is planning on coercing an acceptance of his suit cannot succeed since I am already promised to another."

Richard shook his head in frustration. "I do not know how you are in danger, but I suspect it all hinges on this secret." He turned expectantly to his mother. "Would you agree?"

Lady Matlock nodded slowly. "I know some, but I do not know all. I had not credited what I have heard as truth but as mere gossip; however…" Her voice trailed off.

The three cousins sat in silence, waiting for her to continue. Her brow furrowed and she tapped her lip with her finger as she thought. Finally, she sighed. "Perhaps it is best if I just tell you all I have heard with the caution, of course, that what I know is from secondary sources, so it may or may not be valid." She scowled. "I do not like to gossip. In fact, I despise it. It is not right and holds the power to harm innocent individuals."

Anne, Darcy, and Richard nodded their understanding.

"I am quite certain," she continued, "that the most damning parts of the story are fabricated, but it does not have to be true to be damaging. It needs only to be thought plausible." She sighed again as if resigning herself to the distasteful task of relating unpleasant news. "When you peel away all the details and get to the bare facts, there was scandal surrounding Catherine's marriage. According to James, it was a patched up job. An acceptable choice was forced upon her when she was found in a compromising position with another unacceptable choice. Anne would be tainted by this scandal should she ever come out in London, for there is some question as to whom her father might be."

She turned to Anne. "Although neither of us believes your father is anyone other than Louis de Bourgh, this rumour is the reason your uncle and I have never pushed to give you a proper come out. It is also why your father stipulated in his papers his wish for you to look for a husband outside of London." Her eyes filled with tears. "And why he wishes for you to marry someone in need of an estate. Had Catherine's first choice been a landed gentleman, she may have been allowed to marry for love. Your father loved your mother...not at first, but eventually...;he often regretted the fact that he could not give her the happiness which was taken from her."

Anne dabbed at her eyes. "How tragic! My poor mother!"

"Indeed," agreed Richard.

A scratching at the door interrupted any further conversation.

"My apologies, my lady," said Kellet as he entered the room. "But, there is some information of which you may wish to be apprized." He stood and waited for permission to continue.

"Of course, if you deem it worthy of my notice, it must be so," said Lady Matlock.

"Mr. Collins had come to call on her ladyship."

"At this late hour?" Lady Matlock's eyes grew wide in surprise.

"He was summoned."

"To what purpose?"

He looked quickly at Darcy. "It concerns one of the guests at the parsonage."

"Is he with Lady Catherine?" Lady Matlock was on her feet.

"Not yet, my lady. He is about to arrive. I spied his approach through the window."

"So, there is time for me to intercept him?"

"There is, your ladyship, but I see it doing very little good." He glanced about nervously. "It is not my place to say, but the man has very little sense. He will do whatever his patroness commands." He shifted slightly. "Might I speak freely, my lady?"

"Of course."

"Lady Catherine has instructed the grooms to have a carriage ready at first light. I believe she intends to have Miss Bennet removed from the parsonage, but not until after the young lady has been sufficiently remonstrated by her cousin. As I see it, my lady, the young miss has done nothing to deserve such treatment. I do not know the best plan to prevent this unpleasantness, but I will do whatever you ask."

He turned to Mr. Darcy. "I fear, sir, that letters will be, if they are not already being, written to the young lady's father. I should think your attendance on him before such communication is received may be the only way to prevent his displeasure with a match between yourself and his daughter."

"I shall call at the parsonage straight away," said Lady Matlock. "Darcy you will attend me. You must speak to Miss Bennet regarding your interview with her father. Indeed, Miss Bennet must be removed from the parsonage." She looked to Mr. Kellet and spoke softly. "Is Mr. Collins given to violence?"

"He may lock her in her room and restrict her actions, but I do not believe him capable of harming her."

"And his wife? Would she suffer should I insist on Miss

Bennet attending me at the dower house?" She clapped her hands. "Yes, that is it. She should be moved to the dower house this very night."

"As you request, my lady. Mrs. Collins will be able to deal most effectively with her husband. I am certain she will help him to see a need of not angering the Earl of Matlock, my lady." He gave her a sly smile.

"Just so. My husband would be very displeased if his wife and niece were slighted." She chuckled. "Thank you, Kellet. You will stand without the door of their meeting for me while I am out?"

"Of course, my lady. I shall give you a report as soon as you have returned." He bowed to take his leave.

A footman entered as the butler exited. "Your carriage is waiting, my lady."

Richard could not suppress a small burst of laughter as a maid entered, carrying his mother's outerwear. "He is a most efficient butler, is he not?"

"That he is," she agreed. "It will serve you well to befriend him." She smiled as Darcy's man entered with his coat and hat. "Darcy, I shall await you in the carriage. And Richard and Anne, please try to look like a young couple in love ought to look when you pass Mr. Collins in the hallway. He must see something to cause him to wonder about the two of you." She began to head out the door. "Kiss her if you must," she called over her shoulder.

Chapter 9

Anne turned to Richard when his mother and Darcy had left the room. "Well, what are we to do?" She threw her hands up in frustration. "She is determined to have her way, is she not?"

Richard wound his arms about her from behind and pulled her against him. He could feel her body trembling with emotion. "You must not allow yourself to become overly distraught. We knew she would not take the news of your refusal to marry Darcy well."

"I can bear her displeasure, but I will not allow her to harm another. Miss Elizabeth does not deserve such treatment." She turned in his arms and looked up at him. "As much as I would wish for her to come to her senses on her own, I must tell her of our betrothal. We must attack before she has a chance to fire." She sucked in a quick breath as she heard a knock and the door being answered by Kellet. "Come. We've no time to lose. I am fond of Mrs. Collins, but her husband is insufferable. He must not be told of anything regarding Miss Elizabeth. He will prattle on and on about propriety and maintaining one's place." She took Richard by the arm and started for her mother's parlour.

She turned as she reached the door to the parlour. "Mr. Collins, I assume you have come to see my mother on a matter of great importance, but I am going to have to ask you to wait a few moments. You will not mind, will you? I need to speak to my mother on a delicate matter." She smiled sweetly. "I am sure my mother would understand if you gave precedence to her daughter."

"Of course, Miss de Bourgh, I would not think of placing my needs ahead of yours. What can my needs be compared to that of the daughter of my gracious patroness. Why just this morning I was saying to Mrs. Collins and my cousin Elizabeth how very fortunate I am to have such a position as I do. Lady Catherine is so condescending and —."

"Mr. Collins," Anne interrupted. "I really must see my mother."

The man clamped his lips together and nodded before taking a seat on a bench a short distance down the hall.

Anne breathed deeply. "Ready?" she asked Richard. He nodded and opened the door.

"Anne!" Lady Catherine sat in her chair near the fire. "What are you doing here? I am expecting a caller."

"I know, and it is a pleasure to see you as well, Mother." Anne led Richard to the settee across from her mother.

"What have you done to your hair, and why are you leading him about by the hand?"

Anne sat down, keeping Richard's hand firmly grasped in her own. She gave him a little tug indicating he should also sit. She pulled his hand into her lap and covered it with her other hand.

He could feel her still trembling ever so slightly. He had never truly realized the strength that resided in her delicate frame. How many times had she had to deal with the machinations of her mother on her own? Never again, he promised himself.

"I am not leading him around by the hand, Mother. I am holding his hand because I wish to." Her mother's brow knit slightly in question.

"And my hair must have gotten dishevelled when we were kissing."

Richard coughed to cover a chuckle.

Lady Catherine's eyes grew wide, and her mouth hung open for a moment before she snapped it shut.

"I have come to a decision, Mother," Anne continued before her mother could find her voice. "I am going to marry Richard. He needs an estate and is willing to take on Rosings and me."

Lady Catherine's face grew red. "I will not have my daughter marrying his son after what he did to me." She sputtered. "I will not have it."

"You have no say in the matter, Mother. My decision

is made." She stood. "I shall give you one week to become accustomed to the idea before the banns shall be read for the first time. Mr. Collins awaits you in the hall. You will, of course, wish to have him made aware of his duty to call them."

She still held Richard's hand, and he felt the tremor beginning to increase. He slid an arm around her protectively. "Anne has had a very trying day, and I would not wish for her to become ill because of it. I do not know what you hold against my father, but hear me and hear me well, I am not he. I have made a promise to protect your daughter, and I will stand by my word. No one shall harm her, not even you." He felt Anne relax just a bit in his hold as he continued. "You shall not cause trouble for her, her friend or Darcy. Miss Bennet will be joining Anne and my mother at the dower house. You may tell Mr. Collins of the honour bestowed upon his cousin by Lady Matlock." He waited for her reply.

"I shall do no such thing! I may not have any say in this decision, but I will not just step aside."

"Very well," said Richard. "I will inform Mr. Collins myself and tell him you have unfortunately fallen ill. I shall, of course, send for my father. He will be able to care for you while my mother and I tend to Anne at the dower house. What with her delicate constitution, her removal to the dower house will become even more imperative." He gave her the same look he would have given to an unwilling underling in his command, a look which told them worse was to follow should they decide against following his orders. He watched her face redden and her eyes narrow.

"Take care, Aunt. Do you truly wish for your parson to hear discontent in your home? He is just without in the hall awaiting his interview."

Her jaw clenched, and she huffed.

"One must always do what is needed to preserve the family's reputation," she spat before taking her seat. "Do what you will. My particular happiness has never mattered to anyone in this family. Why should I hope for that to change now?"

Richard started at the vehemence in her voice. He looked questioningly at Anne, but she could only lift a shoulder, helpless to understand the source of her mother's anger. He smiled at her reassuringly before he released her from his grasp and took a seat across from his aunt.

"I do not know of what you speak. While you may refuse to believe the truth of this statement, my father has always longed for your happiness. I have heard him say as much many times. I do not know what has happened in the past; perhaps I wish to know; perhaps I do not." He leaned towards her and lowered his voice to a more soothing tone, one he had used on more than one occasion to calm an angry or fearful soldier. "The past has happened, and it cannot be undone. I can only speak to and work towards the future. You placed a chess piece in a precarious position and charged me, no matter the cost, to protect your daughter not as the pawn which represented her but as the most valuable piece on the board. Is that still your desire? Do you still wish for her to be protected as the most valuable, or shall I put you in that place as you are asking me to do?"

She blinked, her head jerked back ever so slightly, and her brows drew together as she contemplated his question.

"Aunt Catherine, my desire is not to see you unhappy, but I will put your daughter's happiness above anyone's, including yours. How high will the price of such an action be? Shall there be a rift between us? The choice is entirely yours. However, I will ask one more thing. What are your chances for happiness if you are estranged from your daughter and her family?" He rose slowly as she pondered his words. "I will not hear your answer until the morning. Consider your decision carefully." Extending a hand to Anne, he led her from the room.

~*~*~*~*~*~

"Your meeting with Miss Bennet was a success?" Richard first placed a kiss on his mother's cheek and then one on Anne's before taking his regular seat at the table.

Darcy cleared his throat and lifted a brow while trying to hide a grin.

Richard shook his head. "I have greeted Anne in such a fashion all of my life, Darcy. I do not intend to stop doing so now."

"My meeting with Miss Bennet was successful." Lady Matlock turned to Darcy. "You know I will turn a blind eye to small improprieties such as a kiss of greeting, but only if the lady is betrothed to the gentleman. I assume you will be joining those ranks shortly."

Richard nearly choked on his coffee. "Are you off to Hertfordshire today, Darcy?"

Darcy's cheeks had taken on a rosy hue. "I am."

"And are you certain of her acceptance?" Anne placed her tea cup on the table and gave him an amused look.

"I have received her acceptance this morning."

"An early walk in the groves?" Richard asked.

"Indeed." Darcy placed his empty cup on the table. "I needed to know if my trip to Hertfordshire was warranted. Do you wish for me to remain at Rosings until all are settled into the dower house?"

"If you would stay long enough to be party to this morning's conference with our aunt, I should think you could be off with enough time to reach town at an acceptable hour. You had not planned to reach Hertfordshire today, had you?"

"No, no. I had hoped to call on Bingley while in town, and Miss Elizabeth has given me a letter to deliver to her relations. I also wish to extend an invitation for Miss Bennet to travel with Georgiana when she comes for the house party." He paused. His eyebrows rose as an idea formed in his mind. "Perhaps, I shall stay an extra day and escort them myself."

"You would spend an extra day away from Miss Elizabeth?" The colonel's face wore an expression of disbelief. "You shall not become unpleasantly impatient and torment the poor ladies as you travel?"

Darcy smiled. "I shall not promise to be patient or completely content, but I do believe I can act the gentleman for a few hours knowing the prize at the end of the journey. Besides, it would give me time to meet with Wetherald about my offer concerning your commission. I should like to see the matter settled quickly. The banns for your wedding will be read soon?"

"Sunday next," said Anne. "We have given mother a week to reconcile herself to the idea before they begin to be read. It merely means our wedding will be one week later than I should like, but — "

"One week later. Such nonsense," said Lady Catherine as she entered the room. "I do not see why we need to wait an extra week to begin publishing the banns. Whatever trifling ailment seemed to plague me last evening has passed." She gave a meaningful look to Richard, who nodded his acceptance of her change of position. "I shall call upon the parsonage to inform Mr. Collins of the change in plans."

She strode to the table and took her place waving for the footman to pour her tea. "That shall be all," she dismissed him. "See that we are not disturbed."

The four other occupants of the room looked at her with varying degrees of shock on their faces.

"I do not know why you all must sit with your mouths agape. It is very unbecoming, I must say." She sipped her tea. "Richard made an excellent point at the end of his lecture last night. My chance at happiness was snatched from me by overbearing relations, and it seems I have become very much like them. I shall not stand in the way of my daughter's happiness any longer." She placed her cup carefully on the saucer, studying it as she did so. "I must apologize, Anne. I have been bitter for so long, and the choice has always been mine. It is as Richard said. I shall not be happy if you are not happy, and it is only I who can choose to accept things as they are or remain a cantankerous, lonely old woman. I do know how indomitably stubborn a Fitzwilliam male can be — nearly as stubborn as a Fitzwilliam female," she paused to chuckle, "and I dare say Richard would be true to his word and pack me off to some distant port if necessary to have his way."

She looked at the faces which stared back at her in disbelief. "I am not fit for bedlam, if that is what you are thinking. I know it is a sudden turnabout, but a turnabout it is. I have made my choice and am moving forward. How is it you said it, Richard? The past is in the past? And that is where it shall stay."

"And you are certain of this, Catherine?" questioned Lady Matlock. "You are not just taking the role expected of you for the sake of the family?"

"Good heavens, no!" Lady Catherine shook her head. "I have spent far too many years doing as the family expects. Is not a lady in her dotage allowed to do the unexpected? In three weeks, I shall hand over the care of Rosings to the younger set and shall begin to take my ease."

Anne regarded her mother carefully. "Are you quite sure, Mother?"

Lady Catherine smiled at her. "I am. I spent many hours considering what was in my heart. It was not a pleasant task, I can assure you. I have tried with great success to ignore what was there for many years, to deny myself pleasure of any kind, to refuse to allow myself to feel an attachment to anyone or anything, save this home and you, but even there, I have not really formed a proper attachment." She lifted her shoulders sadly. "I feared the pain which comes when something dear to you is wrenched away. I have been a coward, and my heart spoke to me of that very clearly as I pondered it last night."

She rose and walked the length of the room, coming to stop at the window. "I once felt that pain. It is shattering and oppressive and all consuming. It is an agony that if given time to run free in your mind will drive you to the brink of yourself. It was by locking away my heart and refusing to hear it that I — and you — survived. It was because of you I survived."

"What do you mean?" asked Anne.

Lady Catherine drew a breath and turned to face the room. "During my first season, I fell madly in love with a young gentleman. He was beneath me in status but had such a promising future that I knew if I but waited, his success and the wealth which would accompany it would one day sway my father's opinion. We would marry and live happily ever after." She paused. "Yes, as most young girls are, I was a romantic. I know that is difficult to believe to see me now."

She ran her hand along the sideboard as she walked back and forth in front of it. "I told no one save my closest friends — Mrs. Barrows, as you know her, and your uncle, my brother James — we were so very close back then. But somehow, my father became aware of where my affections lay. He, of course, was furious. He refused to allow me even the smallest of freedoms, so that he might know of every interaction I had with every person. It made me all the more determined to have my way, to follow where my heart led. I thought I had managed to contact the gentleman discreetly. So determined was I to follow my heart that I had made arrangements to flee with him one night to Gretna Green. I knew, in doing so, I would lose all standing in society, that I would not receive a farthing of my dowry, and that I would be cut off from my family. But to me the price seemed to pale compared to the prospect of living my life without him."

She shook her head in bewilderment. "To this day, I have no idea how my father found out about my plan or how I became embroiled in a potential scandal which tore me away from my love." Her fingers drummed a pattern on the top of the sideboard as she thought. "I have my suspicions, which have led to the difficulties between James and me."

"Which he denies," said Lady Matlock.

Lady Catherine gave her a small smile. "I attended a ball at the home of Mrs. Barrows' parents. It was a lavish affair. Anyone who was anyone was there. My father had several approved matches in attendance, and I was instructed to spend a minimum of one dance with each. If I did not...well...my father was not above more severe punishment than having my every move watched. I may have found myself locked in my room or worse. As it happened, I ended up with worse." She swallowed and blinked.

"I remember dancing several dances and then scooting off to a quiet room to refresh myself. I sat in that room with my glass of punch in hand and kicked off my slippers. I remember nothing beyond that until sometime later when I was awakened by my father's angry voice. I found my hair all askew and my clothing was disheveled. I was on the couch with my head on the shoulder of the man I planned to marry. He had not been at the ball, yet there he was, looking as bewildered as I at our circumstances. My father, of course, would hear none of our pleading. He threw the man out and threatened him with ruin or worse should he ever be seen near me again, and me, I was locked away in my room for the length of time it took to secure a special license. Then, with horse whip at the ready should I refuse, I was informed I was to marry a man of my father's choosing. He was a man of importance to my father's political position and would receive an estate and a knighthood for saving my reputation."

She took her seat. "I had no choice. I knew to refuse would not just earn me one beating but a lifetime of mistreatment. My father was not known for his patience and kindness. So, I married your father. I became with child almost immediately, but I was not well. My mind was in such a state of despair that the doctors feared not only for my life but also that of my unborn child. When I heard them speaking with my husband, I determined I could not take the life of a child, though I did pray mine would be taken in childbirth. It was not, and because of my poor health, you were born early. They did not expect you to live, but you did. Your determination to survive gave rise to my own determination to persevere."

"Catherine," Lady Matlock spoke softly. "Have you ever noted the wide scar on James' temple?"

Lady Catherine nodded.

"When he heard about what had happened at the ball, he went to see your father while you were shut in your room. He attempted to convince your father not to force you to marry. He even volunteered alternate solutions to any possible scandal, but his father would not hear it. In the course of their discussion, a vase was thrown. That is how he got the scar and why he was unable to attend your wedding." She smiled at her husband, who had entered the room during her explanation.

"Catherine." He bowed a greeting. "I took the liberty of requesting hot tea. I hope you do not mind." He took a roll from the side board and popped a piece of it into his mouth. "Travel does affect one's appetite." He took a chair near his wife. "Lovely to see you, my dear."

"And you, my love."

"You were telling about my scar. Was there a reason?"

"Mother just told us of how she came to marry my father," said Anne. She looked a bit pale and disconcerted.

"Ah, I see. And are you well?" He cocked his head to one side and studied her face.

"I believe I am; though, it is all rather shocking."

He nodded and seemingly satisfied that she was indeed well, shifted his attention to his sister. "And you, Catherine. Are you well?"

"I hardly know. But you truly care that I am, do you not?" Her eyes searched his.

"I always have," he said softly.

Her eyes filled with tears, and she sought her handkerchief. "You did not tell father about Adrian?"

"I promised you I would not. I am a man of my word."

"So then how did he know?"

"Muriel, my dear sister. She is the only other who knew of Cranfield."

"Muriel?"

He nodded. "You know I have never trusted her and for good reason. After you married, she set her cap for our brother."

"Our brother?"

"Indeed. She even had the support of our father for a time, but John would not hear of it." Finishing his roll, he brushed the crumbs from his fingers. "There was a rather loud discussion that I happened upon. Father wanted an alliance with Leighton for some reason. Some foolishness about having good hunting grounds which would afford fabulous opportunities for rustication with his political cohorts."

"He wanted John to marry Muriel for her father's hunting grounds?"

Lady Catherine's brows drew together in question. "Did anything our father did ever make sense?"

"It made perfect sense. It was always to strengthen his position politically and to increase the family coffers. It was just never for the reason he gave." He leaned toward his sister, his gaze intent on her, and his voice soft. "That is not all I heard of the discussion. I also heard John shout something about 'after what she did to Catherine?' but the rest was lost to the crash of another vase. Thankfully, John's reflexes are better. It merely damaged the door and not his head."

Lady Catherine's eyes grew wide. The shock of hearing that her dearest friend had been the source of her unhappiness was evident in her features. Anne had just begun to worry about if it all had not been too much for her mother when the door opened, and her mother assumed her normal expression.

"Pardon me, my lady." Kellet stepped into the room and closed the door softly behind him. He took several steps toward the group who sat around the table and lowered his voice to speak. "Mrs. Barrows, Miss Barrows, and the young Mr. Barrows to see you and Miss de Bourgh, my lady. I have placed them in the sitting room, but if you are not feeling up to company..." He let the idea hang in the air as he waited her response.

"A moment please."

Kellet nodded and stepped back to stand by the door.

Lady Catherine looked thoughtful. "I made the appointment before we spoke last night, Anne. I thought Mr. Barrows...well, it does not signify what I thought. It was the silly notion of a bitter old woman. I suppose we must entertain them for a few minutes at least. Do you not think?"

Anne nodded. "It seems the appropriate thing to do. However, we do have much to do with the removal to the dower house and the arrival of Lord Matlock." She lifted a brow and gave her mother a small smile before taking a final sip of tea and standing. "You gentlemen will attend us, will you not?"

"As if nothing has changed since last we met?" Lady Catherine questioned.

"Indeed. I believe it would be best."

"Would you give me a few minutes to speak with my father and Darcy before joining you?" asked Richard.

Anne smiled and patted his forearm, which lay on the table. "Of course, but please come to my rescue soon. I find Mr. Barrows to be a dreary conversationalist, and his sister, well, I am sure she will be hoping to see a gentleman or two." She laughed. "Unfortunately, there are no available gentlemen to be duly impressed by her charms."

Chapter 10

Two days later, Anne watched through the breakfast room window at the dower house for Richard to return from his ride. Her tea grew cold as it stood untouched on the table. It was not like him to be late for breakfast. A sense of dread settled in her stomach, causing her to feel like expelling the bit of toast she had managed to eat.

"Anne." Lady Matlock placed an arm around her shoulders. "He is merely late. Come, you must eat."

Anne sank into her chair and dutifully took up her cup. "I cannot shake the feeling that all is not well."

"We could go for a drive after we eat," offered Elizabeth. "I know we cannot access all the trails he might ride, but we could occasionally stop and walk a bit."

Anne gave her a grateful smile. She was glad to have a friend such as Elizabeth. "I would like that."

"Then it is settled." Lady Matlock rose to have the phaeton readied.

"Do you miss Darcy?" Anne asked softly while her aunt was outside the room.

A blush stained Elizabeth's cheeks, and she laughed nervously. "I do."

"It is silly, is it not?" Anne broke off a small piece of toast. "I would not have thought to miss Richard so just two days ago." She placed the bread in her mouth and chewed. "Everything changes when your heart is engaged." She pushed her plate away. "Here I am unable to eat and missing him when he has been gone a few hours, and you have been without Darcy's presence for two days and will not see him until the morrow. I should be more calm like you."

Elizabeth placed her cup on the table and wiped her mouth with her napkin. "If Mr. Darcy were expected and had not returned, I would not be so calm. As it is, I find myself peering out the window, watching the road far more than I should." She took up a muffin. "And unlike you, I currently find the waiting has increased my appetite. I fear if Mr. Darcy is gone for too long, I may not retain my figure."

Anne laughed. "I can ask cook to pack a basket for our excursion if you wish."

Elizabeth shook her head and smiled. "No. I have eaten enough to sustain both me and you."

"My lady," a maid scurried into the room just as Lady Matlock returned. "Stewart says the colonel's horse has returned without him."

"Without him?" Lady Matlock halted mid-step.

"Yes, ma'am." The maid twisted her apron. "The horse appeared at the stables without Colonel Fitzwilliam. Stewart says the grooms have begun a search, but he wished for you to be made aware of the facts, my lady."

"The phaeton cannot be made ready, my lady." Randall, the butler, entered the room. He gave the maid a disapproving look.

"I am sorry, Mr. Randall." The maid ducked her head. "Cook said to make haste, and I could not find you, sir."

His look softened, but he motioned with his head that she should leave the room. She dropped a curtsey and hurried from the room ahead of him.

"Thank you, Randall." Anne moved to the window. She could just see the stables if she stood at the correct angle.

"He may have just gotten separated from his horse." Lady Matlock stood next to her. "We must not imagine the worst until there is no other option."

~*~*~*~*~*~

Richard lay on the ground looking at the clouds as they floated past. He attempted to pull himself to a seated position, but the world was spinning far too fast for him to stay upright. Pain shot through his leg. He wiggled his toes inside his boot. The motion only increased the pain. Broken. It was quite likely broken. He sighed. How was he to return to the dower house if he could not hold himself upright and had only one good leg?

He turned his head to the side and watched as his horse galloped away. Hopefully, the animal would find its way home, prompting a search. He closed his eyes even as he tried to fight the urge to sleep. He knew he needed to stay alert. As he lay focusing his thoughts on staying awake, he heard a rustling behind him.

"Do you think 'e be dead?" asked a voice.

"Ain't never seen a dead man afore," said a second voice.

"Barrows ain't gonna be happy if 'e ain't dead."

"Barrows only said 'e needed 'im out of the way to woo the girl. Dead or injured, 'e be out of the way."

"Do you think we should run 'im through? Just to make sure 'e be out of the way?"

"I ain't killin' no one. Scaring an 'orse be one thing. Sticking a man be something else completely." The second man's voice grew softer as he moved away from Richard. He strained to hear what they were saying.

"Ain't you gonna stay to see what 'appens to 'im?" There was a shuffling of feet as the first man followed the second.

"Nah. Wagon's comin' tonight. Gotta be ready. More money in crapauds than in scaring 'orses."

Crapauds? Frenchmen? Richard's eyes flew open. He attempted to move his head to see the men who had been talking, but they were gone.

He no longer needed to fight his fatigue. His mind was

fully alert now. Were Frenchmen entering the country or was it just goods? He struggled once more into a sitting position. The world tilted and turned a bit before righting itself. He closed his eyes and opened them again. The spinning returned for a moment but quickly passed. He focused on a nearby tree. If he could just get to that tree, perhaps he could find a branch that could be used to help him hobble back to Rosings. He knew standing without assistance was not an option, so carefully, without moving his injured leg too much, he positioned himself to crawl on his hands and one good knee to the tree, dragging his leg behind him.

"I see him!" A shout rang out. "Over here." Richard looked for the sound of the voice and breathed a sigh of relief as he recognized one of Rosings' grooms.

"Can I help you, sir?"

"You had best sit for a bit, John," said Richard noticing how hard the young man was breathing. "We would do better to wait for at least one other to join us. I am afraid my leg is broken, and I will require a couple of strong bodies upon which to lean." He nodded his head toward the grass next to him. "You are a fast runner."

"Thank you, sir. I have four brothers. One learns to be fast if he wishes to claim anything before the others."

"And which are you? The eldest or the youngest?"

"The middle, sir. Two older and two younger."

"Ah, so you had to overtake the elders and learn to be pleasing enough to outshine the younger brothers?"

"Indeed." The young groom laughed. "Although to be found in the middle is a fine place to be if you wish to not be noticed."

"I see we are about to be joined by reinforcements." Richard looked up to see two more men hurrying in their direction. "Can you find two sturdy sticks about the length of my leg from knee to foot?"

"I can, sir." John rose to do as he was asked, but paused to retrieve something from his pocket. "I have a bit of rope, sir. It is not very thick, but it is strong." He handed it to Richard. "It should be enough to secure your leg between the branches."

Richard smiled at him. "You are well prepared."

"Thank you, sir." The groom bowed. "I shall not be long, sir."

~*~*~*~*~*~

Anne sat next to his bed when he opened his eyes. He moved his leg and winced. "It is nearly worth the pain to see your face upon waking."

"It was not worth the worry, I can assure you." Anne wiped his brow with a damp cloth. "Twenty minutes late returning from your ride and two days of lying here insensible and burning with fever."

"Two days?" He blinked and looked at her in confusion. "I did not just return?"

Darcy laughed. "No, cousin, it is as Anne said. We have been quite worried about you."

"Darcy? When did you return?"

"Yesterday as planned."

"So, it really has been two days?"

Anne sighed in exasperation.

He caught her hand and held it to his chest. "It is rather difficult to believe you have missed two days without a trace of a memory of them." He lifted her hand and kissed it while giving her an apologetic look.

"I suppose you are right," she conceded. "I am glad you have returned." She glanced at Darcy, who turned away so she could place a kiss on Richard's lips. "The house party has been less than festive while we waited for you. I shall be happy to have your company for conversation instead of Mr. Barrows'."

"Barrows is here?" Richard pulled himself up in the bed. "I do not remember his name on the list."

"He is not residing here or at Rosings. He merely appears to call on me each day and inquire after your health."

Richard snorted. "He will be disappointed I have survived."

"What do you mean?" asked Darcy.

"He was the one behind my accident. Hired two men to spook my horse. They thought I was dead. One of them suggested running me through to make sure I was, but neither felt it was worth the bother. Apparently, I needed to be out of the way so Barrows could court Anne." He groaned as he tried to shift to a more comfortable seated position. It was then he noticed Anne's pale face and shocked expression.

"He...he tried to...to...kill you?" She stammered. "And he sits in my house playing the part of a concerned neighbour?" She stood and paced the room. "The scoundrel!"

"Anne," Richard called to her. "He did not succeed."

"But he could have."

"While that is in the realm of possibilities, it is not reality." He patted the chair next to the bed. "Please do not get overwrought by something that did not happen."

She gave him a slight scowl but returned to take her seat next to him. "I have very good reasons to be overwrought. Do you remember how my father died?" She looked between Darcy and Richard.

"An illness, was it not?" asked Darcy.

She shook her head. "He was thrown from his horse. One day, it returned to the stables without him, just as yours did. When the grooms found him, he was unconscious but breathing. He developed a fever much like you did, Richard, but for him it was too much. His injuries were too severe, and he succumbed to the fever." She brushed the hair from Richard's forehead. "He was an excellent horseman. I had seen him keep his seat when a horse was rearing. I have never believed it to be an accident."

"You think he was murdered?" Darcy sat on the edge of the bed.

"I do, but I have no proof. I do not even know who would want him dead or why."

Richard scrubbed his face with his hands. "I have truly missed two days?"

"Yes," said both Darcy and Anne.

"Then it is too late." He covered his eyes with one of his hands and allowed his head to rest against the headboard. "One of the men mentioned a wagon and money from the French. But the wagon was to come in that night. And I can do nothing while lying here in this bed with a bad leg."

"I could ask Kellet to come see you," suggested Darcy. "Your father insisted he be stationed here. He may know something."

At that Richard brightened. "Yes, yes, he might know something. And was Alcock able to attend the party?"

"He is here."

"Good." Richard clapped his hands and then rubbed them together in eager anticipation. "Then send both him and Kellet up to see me, and perhaps one of them could bring some food."

"I am afraid you shall have to endure the doctor first,"

said Darcy. "He was sent for as soon as you started to rouse, and I do believe that is his voice I hear below."

Richard groaned.

"I will stay and make sure he does not give you any medicine until after you have had your conference with Kellet and Alcock." Darcy patted Richard's good leg. "You have been ill. Even you need some time to recover."

Richard rolled his eyes.

"He is right," said Anne as she stood to leave. "You need rest, but after I see to having some food sent to you, I will inform Colonel Alcock and Mr. Kellet of your desire to see them."

Richard caught her by the hand before she could move away. "Is Barrows here?"

"I believe he is."

"You will be careful?"

"I will."

"Good." He drew her back to sit on the edge of his bed. "Darcy, it might be best if you greet the doctor and inform him of my improvements before he sees me."

Darcy leaned against the door frame, a playful smile on his face. "I can tell him just as well when he arrives in the room."

"Darcy." Richard growled.

"Yes?"

"Go away."

Darcy laughed. "I shall inform the doctor of your condition." He turned before closing the door. "It will not take long," he warned.

Chapter 11

"How is he?" Elizabeth, who was waiting at the bottom of the stairs, slipped her arm through Anne's.

"He is alert." A smile lit Anne's face while tears slipped silently down her cheeks. "Darcy told you to wait here for me?"

"He did, though I have been anxious to see you." Elizabeth pulled her close. "Now, tell me. Besides the injured leg, does he suffer any ill effects of his accident?"

A small joyful laugh bubbled out of Anne. "No. He appears to have just woken from a sound sleep. It is quite remarkable. Oh, Elizabeth, I am so relieved."

"As well you should be. It has been a harrowing ordeal."

"Mr. Kellet," said Anne as he approached them. "Colonel Fitzwilliam asked to speak with you, but first he requires some broth and bread."

"Right away, Miss de Bourgh." A faint smile appeared on his face. "I am glad to hear it, miss," he added softly. Then, with a flick of his hand he summoned a footman and sent him scurrying to the kitchen. "Mr. Barrows and Miss Barrows have just arrived."

Anne dried her eyes. "Perhaps my red eyes will drive him away. The Lord knows nothing else has worked. He is most determined."

Elizabeth chuckled. "That he is, but he seems harmless enough."

Anne shook her head. "Appearances can be deceiving, my dear." She pulled Elizabeth into a small alcove near the front door. "Richard's accident was arranged," she whispered, "by Mr. Barrows."

Elizabeth gasped.

"It is true." Anne paused. "I will tell you more once our guests leave. For now, we must be on our guard, and I will do my best to discourage his suit." She drew Elizabeth out of the alcove and toward the drawing room.

Lady Matlock greeted them at the door. "I was just going to check on my son. He is truly well?"

"He is." Anne placed a hand on her aunt's arm. "Thank you for entertaining my guests while I sat with him."

"At his side is more your place than mine, and I am happy to give that place to you. I will go up now and see him."

"The doctor is with him now, and he has requested that I send his friend up to see him."

Lady Matlock chuckled. "He always was a quick healer

and a restless patient. I shall not be long, perhaps five minutes, and then he can have his conference with his friend. He needs rest, whether he agrees with the fact or not."

"He does not," said Anne.

"He never does," said Lady Matlock. "He never does."

Anne laughed and entered the room.

"May I assume by your happy expression that your cousin is doing well?" asked Miss Barrows. "I had hoped to hear encouraging news about him, and I do hope I am not to be disappointed. I have missed seeing him in company these last days."

Anne smiled as politely as she could at the young lady. Indeed, Miss Barrows had become very interested in the well-being of Richard when it became obvious that Darcy's affections lay elsewhere. However, she had been equally as attentive to Richard's friend Colonel Alcock, especially when she had learned his father was a marquess. "Colonel Fitzwilliam is doing very well. So well, in fact, that he is going to take a source of pleasure from us for a while. Colonel Alcock, he is most anxious to see you."

"I am surprised he did not just push the doctor away and hobble down the stairs. It is not like him to miss out on any entertainment." Alcock chuckled. "The stories I could tell you, Miss de Bourgh, but I shall wait until Fitz is able to defend himself." Colonel Alcock gave a small parting bow to the ladies.

Anne took a seat on a settee near Miss Barrows and

breathed a small sigh of relief when Elizabeth sat next to her. Mr. Barrows, who had been moving toward her, shifted his route just slightly to take the seat next to his sister.

"You are looking well, Miss de Bourgh," he said.

Anne shook her head. "Thank you for your generosity, sir, but I look far less than well." She enjoyed the look of shock which quickly passed across the gentleman's face. She had grown weary of his fawning and flattery. Since her polite discouragements had fallen on ears unwilling to hear them, perhaps a less subtle approach would do the job. "I have been far to occupied with the condition of my cousin to worry about the trivial matter of my appearance." She heard a small gasping noise next to her and was sure Elizabeth was struggling to contain a laugh.

"Yes, well," Mr. Barrows fumbled with his words for a moment. "Then your ability to look well under such trying circumstances is of greater credit to you."

"I am sure it is." Anne turned from him. "Mr. Bingley, while I was tending to Richard, Darcy mentioned you have an uncle who will be travelling through this area."

Bingley sat forward a bit in his seat. "Indeed, I do. My uncle plans to meet one of his ships at Dover. He has not been pleased with some reports he has received regarding the captain and must speak with the man."

"He is in trade?" Miss Barrows' eyebrows rose, and there was a hint of revulsion in her voice.

"He is." Bingley gave her an appraising look. "My father was also in trade. I am the first to be given the opportunity to become a landed gentleman. Thanks to their success...in trade."

"How fortunate for you."

"It is, is it not? Without his hard work and that of my father, I would not have been able to let Netherfield and would never have met the lovely Miss Bennet and her family." He took Jane's hand and settled back into his chair.

"What do you mean without his hard work? Did not your fortune come as a result of your father's will?" Mr. Barrows cleared his throat and gave a small shake of his head at his sister's question. She lowered her eyes and coloured slightly. "Forgive me. My curiosity has gotten the better of my manners."

"Curiosity has a way of doing that. I have been known to be far more curious than entirely proper at times myself." Bingley laughed lightly. "But to answer your questions, my father's fortune passed to me upon his death with the stipulation that I use it to acquire an estate to secure my son, should I be so fortunate as to have one, in the more respected realm of the landed gentry. My uncle received full ownership of their business, a business that succeeded only through the dedicated efforts of both men. Therefore, my fortune can be credited to not only my father but also my uncle. And, upon his passing, I shall receive his fortune as well since he has never married, and I am his heir."

Miss Barrows blinked. "Oh, so your wealth will increase?" This time, her brother nudged her with his elbow.

"It will, and quite substantially. I will, of course, then be faced with the decision of selling or keeping the business. But, it is not a decision I hope to be faced with for some time."

"Your uncle is welcome to stay here on his journey," Anne said before Miss Barrow could ask any further questions. "It would be much more comfortable than any inn. When do you expect him?"

"He hoped to dine with me tomorrow. I could send an express to the inn he usually frequents in Bromley."

"Oh, yes, you must. He must join us." Anne cast a glance at Mr. Barrows to see how he would receive such information. Much to Anne's delight, Mr. Barrows looked a bit uncomfortable.

"It is a pity we shall not be able to meet him." He said. "I have matters of a pressing nature which must be attended to tomorrow."

"What unfortunate timing for you! Perhaps if Mr. Bingley's uncle is able to stop on his return, you might have the pleasure then." She noted the look of amusement on Bingley's face as Mr. Barrows' eyes grew large, and he stammered his agreement. "And you shall miss our ride through the groves. I have a picnic planned, provided the weather holds." She stood. "But for now, I would be most pleased if you would all join me for a game of pall mall."

~*~*~*~*~*~

Anne tapped her ball, sending it neatly through the wire arch.

"Well done, Miss de Bourgh," said Mr. Barrows as he leaned upon his mallet. "You have beaten me again."

"It does not seem a hard task to do so. Tell me, do you not partake in the activity very often?" He had been following her about the lawn, and his presence was beginning to grate.

He gave her a tight smile. "I do not spend much time playing games. I am more a man of action. My life is not one of ease. I have a profession and not an estate."

"So, an estate would give you a life of ease?" Anne's brows rose. "If it is a well-managed estate, you may be able to spend some time in leisurely pursuits, but it takes much work to allow for the ease of which you speak."

"Indeed. I did not mean to say there was no work involved in the management of an estate." His words had a bit of an edge to them. "But you must admit, most of the working class have very few hours to spend in pleasure."

"Absolutely," agreed Anne. "We all benefit much from those who give of their time and skills to serve others. You, for instance, must allocate time to your studies and the needs of your parishioners. It is a great responsibility and one upon which many rely for guidance. Though you are also one of the fortunate, for your living is not inconsequential and allows for freedoms and luxuries that even my mother's parson cannot afford."

"Perhaps if Rosings had a master to run it, it could gain in productivity and the living could be increased."

"Yes," said Anne curtly. "I shall have to look for such a man. Good day, Mr. Barrows." Anne stooped to retrieve her ball.

His hand on her arm stopped her from walking away. "I know of such a man — a man of action who is not unfamiliar with the running of an estate, a man who could provide for and protect you." He ran a finger gently up her arm.

She dropped her ball and removed his hand from her arm. "I will thank you not to touch me in the future. I shall find my own choice, and it will not be you."

His face turned hard. "Choices are not always ours to make. Sometimes they are forced upon us. I would take care if I were you, Miss de Bourgh. Not many men will look twice at a soiled dove."

Anne narrowed her eyes and glared at him. "I am not soiled, and I do not appreciate your insinuation that I am. You are a gentleman and a man of the cloth. Such talk is most unseemly."

He stepped a half step closer and whispered menacingly. "I assure you, Miss de Bourgh, when I report to one and all that you are soiled, it will not be an insinuation. You would do well to consider my offer to run Rosings. At least then when I have my way with you, it shall be as your husband."

"Anne." Elizabeth approached her from behind. "We have played through twice, and I would appreciate a rest. Mr. Bingley has gone to write his express, and Jane has gone to find a book to read in her room. Colonel Alcock has returned, so you may wish to look in on Colonel Fitzwilliam. Colonel Alcock says he was asking for you."

"Asking for you, is he?" Mr. Barrows said softly. "It seems you and your cousin are very close — hopefully not closer than is entirely proper, or perhaps my assessment is true." His eyes swept up and down her person before he bowed to take his leave.

"Mr. Barrows." Her words stopped him. "You will leave, and you will not return. Your sister may visit if she would like, but you shall not set foot in my home or garden again." She turned on her heel and taking Elizabeth by the arm, returned to the house.

~*~*~*~*~*~

Anne attempted to let go of Elizabeth's arm as they entered the house, but Elizabeth held her firmly and directed her to the stairs.

"I am well," insisted Anne.

"I am sure you are, my dear, but I am not going to be well until I know what that man said to you. And, instead of having you repeat it to me and then again to Colonel Fitzwilliam, I am attending you to his room."

They stopped outside of Richard's room. "You will tell him what was said, will you not?" She knocked softly on the door before Anne could answer.

Anne peeked around the door as it opened, anxious to see if Richard was still awake. She breathed a sigh as she saw him sitting up in the bed and looking awake and even comfortable. "How are you feeling, Richard?"

"Bored." He patted the bed next to him. "Come keep me company." He frowned just a bit when she took the chair next to the bed. "Are your guests enjoying themselves?"

"Georgiana and Maria have tucked themselves away all day. I have not seen them, but I have heard music and giggling, so I am sure they are enjoying themselves. Jane is currently reading, while Mr. Bingley writes an express to invite his uncle to join us tomorrow. Colonel Alcock has been with you until lately and mentioned something about riding." She smoothed her skirt and cast a glance in Elizabeth's direction. "And the Barrows have left. I do not expect them to return."

Richard's eyebrows rose in surprise. "Indeed? And why, pray tell, will they not be returning?"

"Because I have forbidden it. Well, to clarify, I have only told Mr. Barrows he may not return. His sister is free to call if she wishes. We shall see if her desire to flirt with Colonel Alcock overrides her disdain of trade."

"Disdain of trade?" Darcy asked.

"She was very clear in our conversation with Mr. Bingley about his uncle that she does not approve of those who are in trade," said Elizabeth.

"Is that so?" asked Richard.

"It is," said Anne.

"So, that explains Miss Barrows' reason for possibly returning or not returning, but what of Mr. Barrows?"

Anne again looked at Elizabeth, who urged her on with a small nod of her head. "He spoke in a most inappropriate fashion to me, so I told him he was no longer welcome."

With a small groan, Richard pulled himself up even straighter in the bed. "Exactly how was he inappropriate?"

"Well, he made me an offer. He is quite interested in the position of master of Rosings. Interested enough to take me as a wife."

"You banished him for making an offer of marriage?" asked Darcy.

Anne shook her head firmly. "No, I refused his offer out of hand." She looked at Richard. "Do you promise not to do anything that will cause you further discomfort or injury?"

Richard's heart dropped to his stomach, dread filled

his belly. "I am not sure I am capable of making such a promise, but I shall endeavour to remain calm."

"You shall not be able to remain calm. You may rant, and you may roar, but do not attempt to get out of that bed." Anne gave him a stern glare.

"Anne, will you just tell me."

"He threatened me."

"How?" The dread he had felt a moment ago began to spread, his heart increased its beating, and his head began to throb. He clutched the blankets to keep from tossing them back and getting out of the confounded bed.

"He mentioned ruining me so that I would have no choice but to marry him." Her face felt warm, and she dared not look up from her hands. "Then when he heard that you had requested to see me, he implied that perhaps I was already ruined, and that is when I told him he was no longer welcome in my home or garden."

"I will kill him," Richard growled. "If he utters one rumour about you or lays one finger on you, I will kill him. If it were not for this blasted leg, I would go have a few words with him now."

"You would ruin Alcock's plan," cautioned Darcy.

"Devil take the plan, Darcy. The man has attempted to kill me, and now he has threatened Anne. I care very little about anything else in which he may be involved at the moment."

"You say that now, but in a few hours when you possess a cooler head, you will still wish to know about his other activities." Darcy stood and walked toward the bed. "Think for a moment. Anne, you said he was interested in the running of Rosings, did you not?"

"I did." She wished to ask Darcy why that information was important but recognized his attempt to shift Richard's thoughts. She smiled. They had always been as close as brothers. They knew each other's strengths and weaknesses. One was always looking out for the other.

Richard scowled. "I know what you are about, Darcy."

"Good. Then be of some use and redirect your thoughts without my prodding. Your deductive skills are as necessary to this plan and Anne's safety as your leg, if not more so. And if you will direct your thoughts as you should, I can stop pacing around the room in an effort to capture your attention and go back to sitting beside Miss Elizabeth, who is far prettier company than a cranky old soldier."

Richard huffed. "Oh, go back to your seat, Darcy. You have made your point. And I'll thank you not to call me old."

"You are older than I am," said Darcy taking his seat next to Elizabeth.

"Oh," said Elizabeth with a wink at Richard, "then you must be very old indeed if you are older than Mr. Darcy."? Richard threw his head back and laughed.

"Thank you," mouthed Anne to Elizabeth and Darcy.

Then she turned to Richard. "Now about this plan. I should very much like to hear about it."

Richard stopped laughing and cast a look at his cousin. "Do we tell them?"

Darcy shrugged his shoulders. "Do you really have a choice? You know how stubborn Anne can be when she wishes to know something."

Richard sighed. "Right. Well. This goes no further than this room, and you will not attempt to take part in any of it. If you can agree to those two simple rules, I shall tell you." He waited until he got a nod of agreement from both ladies. Then, he proceeded to lay out the plan.

Chapter 12

"Anne," said Lady Matlock as she entered Anne's room. "Everything is ready. Your guests will be gathering on the lawn soon." She cocked her head to the side and smiled. "You do look lovely, my dear. Pink is very becoming on you." She turned to leave. "And your mother has decided to join us."

"My mother?" Anne turned toward her aunt. "My mother is joining us?" she asked incredulously.

Lady Matlock stood near the door. "She is, as is your uncle. He assures me her attitude is still changed. They have been enjoying each other's company and re-establishing what they once had."

"But my mother does not like to eat out of doors. She claims it is uncivilized and beneath her."

"Well, today it is not, and neither is riding."

"Riding? Mother does not ride."

"Today she does."

Anne shook her head in disbelief. Her mother had said she was a changed woman, but Anne had no idea she would be changed to such an extent. She snatched up her bonnet and followed her aunt to the garden to await her guests.

"Mother, it is a pleasure to see you."

"I would not miss my daughter's celebration of her birth." She stepped closer to Anne and gave her an awkward hug and a peck on the cheek.

"Of course not, Mother, but I expected you for dinner, not the picnic." Anne could not hide her shock.

Lord Matlock chuckled. "Catherine loved nothing better than a picnic when we were young. She was often scolded for taking her tea to the garden."

"I have not been on a picnic in years. It is about time I start enjoying life again, no matter the memories they may unearth." Lady Catherine looked out across the garden as if remembering some fond excursion. "The last picnic I attended was rather secretive. It was one of the times I stole away to see Adrian. In fact, it was the day before the Leightons' ball." She shook her head to clear the memories. "But today is not about what was or could have been; it is about what is. Now, when do we depart?"

"As soon as everyone gathers," replied Lady Matlock.

"I say, it is a nice day for an excursion," declared Bingley as he approached the group. Anne watched as her mother's face grew pale, and she leaned a bit on her brother's arm.

Bingley bowed as he joined them. "Good morning, Miss de Bourgh."

"Good morning, Mr. Bingley."

"Bingley?" Lady Catherine's voice had an odd squeak to it.

"Yes, Mother, this is Mr. Bingley, Darcy's friend. Mr. Bingley, my mother, Lady Catherine."

"Bingley?" Lady Catherine squeaked once more. "A relation to Herbert Bingley?"

"Yes, ma'am. He was my father."

"He was married to Susanna Cranfield?" Lady Catherine swayed.

"Yes, she is my mother, and Miss de Bourgh has been kind enough to invite her brother, who is my uncle, to join us for dinner this evening, though I suspect he will be an early arrival."

"Adrian? Adrian Cranfield?"

"Yes, my lady." Bingley began to look decidedly nervous.

"Mr. Adrian Cranfield will be here, this evening?" Lady Catherine clutched her brother's arm and swayed again. "You....you...look just like him."

Lord Matlock caught her as she swooned. "You there," he called to a footman. "Help me get her to the parlour." Carefully, they carried her into the house and placed her on the couch while a maid scurried to retrieve smelling salts and cool water.

"Was it something I said?" Bingley paced about the room. "I am terribly sorry, although I am not quite sure for what I am sorry." He wrung his hands and sat down in a chair but just on the edge as if he might decide to move again.

Lady Matlock studied Bingley for a few moments. "Catherine is right. You do look a great deal like your uncle."

"I take after mother's side of the family." He ran a hand through his hair. "Do you know my uncle?"

"I do, but not so well as my husband or Lady Catherine does. I did not know Susanna's married name. We did not travel in the same circles."

Bingley gave an amused huff. "I should think not. My father was through and through a tradesman. He had little use for the upper class save to take their money for his services." He looked nervously at Lord Matlock. "I mean no disrespect. I merely share my father's views, which differ from my own."

"If he disliked the upper class so, then why has he stipulated that you use the money he left you to buy an estate?" Jane asked softly.

"My mother and uncle insisted that being a landed gentleman would afford me and my children greater opportunity, opportunities he said that were available only to those who owned a substantial estate."

"Did he ever marry?" asked Lord Matlock.

"My uncle? No. He claimed he had no heart to be engaged. I assume he was crossed in love."

"He was." Lady Catherine attempted to sit, but Anne kept a firm hand on her shoulder. "But not by the lady he loved." She pushed at Anne's hand. "For heaven's sake, Anne, allow me to sit."

Anne refused to relinquish her hold. "Not just yet, Mother. You have only regained your senses. I know from experience that rising too soon after swooning will only precipitate another episode. Be patient."

Lady Catherine huffed but complied. "It was my father."

Bingley looked at her in confusion. "Your father? Forgive me, but I do not understand your meaning."

"My father refused to allow me to marry your uncle."

"Bingley's uncle?" Darcy's eyes grew wide in astonishment. "Bingley's uncle is your lost love?"

Lady Catherine nodded; a tear escaping her eye was quickly dried by Anne.

Darcy shook his head in disbelief. "Of course he is. When you spoke to us recently, you called him Adrian and Uncle James called him Cranfield. I cannot believe I did not put the pieces of information together. If I had been quicker with my thinking, I could have saved you a shock. I am sorry, Aunt Catherine."

"Do you wish for him to not dine with us?" asked Bingley. "I could ride out and meet him."

"No!" Lady Catherine pushed Anne away and sat up. "I would not rescind an invitation; however, I will remove myself if need be. I would greatly like to see him again, but he may not wish to see me."

"I will ride out," said Bingley. "I will not withdraw the invitation, but I will make him aware of all the facts."

"But the picnic. You mustn't miss the picnic. They are such wonderful opportunities for young people to get to know one another." Lady Catherine looked at Jane. "I would not deprive you of your happiness. I shall simply take my dinner with my nephew. Richard will be anxious for company, I am sure."

"I am quite anxious for some already," said Richard as Kellet pushed him into the room.

"Wherever did you find that old bath chair?" asked Anne.

"It was in the attic, Miss," said Kellet.

"He did not make you carry him down the stairs, did he?" Anne gave Richard a stern look.

"No, Miss. Patrick and Nate were of assistance."

"I did not ask to be carried, but they would not give me a crutch so that I could hop down under my own power."

"Three days. Three days and two of those you have been insensible and feverish. You will do yourself harm," Anne scolded.

"I will not do myself harm. Many a soldier rises from his bed mere days after his injury."

"Without relapse or any ill effect?" Anne shook her head.

Colonel Alcock caught a laugh.

Anne turned to him. "I am right, am I not?"

He nodded.

Anne narrowed her eyes and looked once again at Richard. "No crutches until next week. I've not yet recovered from the fright of your accident." She walked to the door of the parlour and called to Kellet. "Please set up the picnic in the side garden." She turned back to the room. "I will not risk having him ride a horse or climb a hill." A ripple of laughter spread around the room.

"I had no intentions of climbing a hill," said Richard with a smile. "Now, would someone please tell me why my aunt needs to eat with me?"

"Bingley's uncle is coming," said Darcy.

"Yes, yes, I know. Anne told me about that last night. But I do not see why that makes a difference. Surely there are enough chairs."

"Bingley's uncle is Adrian Cranfield."

Richard looked at Anne expecting her to continue. Then before she could, he cocked his head to one side and furrowed his brow. "I've heard the name before, have I not?"

Anne nodded and waited for him to piece it together.

"Aunt Catherine called the man she planned to marry

Adrian, and Father called him Cranfield." His eyes grew wide. "That man was Bingley's uncle?"

"He still is Bingley's uncle, and he is arriving later today."

Lady Catherine rose from the couch. "I do not wish to avoid him, but he may wish to avoid me. I believe he was told a story about me which was not entirely true. I would not wish to see someone if I thought I had been ill-used by her. But, enough about me. This is Anne's day, and I will not ruin it with my tale of woe." She smiled at her daughter. "Will Georgiana and Miss Lucas be joining us?"

"Along with Mrs. Ainsley and Mrs. Jenkins," said Anne. "I shall go inform them of our change of plans."

"No, Anne, Miss Elizabeth and I shall go," said Darcy. Richard raised an eyebrow and gave him a smirk. Darcy scowled at him as he offered his arm to Elizabeth. "We'll not be long," he said, which only caused Richard to grin more broadly, and from the look in his eye, Anne was certain he was going to add some teasing comment. However, his remarks were left unsaid as Kellet announced Miss Barrows.

"Miss Barrows," Anne greeted her in surprise. "I was not expecting to see you today."

"I had not thought I would be able to attend, but here I am. Mother said it would be very rude of me not to at least attend the picnic." She turned and smiled at Richard. "It is lovely to see you up and about, Colonel."

"It is good to be somewhere other than my bed," agreed Richard.

"However, due to Richard's lack of mobility, we have decided to have our picnic in the garden. I do hope you will not be too disappointed," said Anne.

"Oh, not at all, I assure you. It is more the company than the location that guarantees the success of any social function."

"Shall we proceed to the garden then?" Lord Matlock offered an arm to both his wife and his sister.

~*~*~*~*~*~

"Miss de Bourgh, would you care to take a turn about the garden with me?" asked Miss Barrows. "The men have taken to discussing war, and I am not fond of such conversation." She wrinkled her nose at the thought, looking very much like a young girl fresh from the schoolroom.

"Of course, Miss Barrows, I will join you." She gave Richard's hand a pat as she left his side.

"You are quite devoted to him," said Miss Barrows.

"I suppose I am," admitted Anne. "But, I believe a wife should feel devotion for her husband, so it is a good sign that I feel that now even though we are not yet married. Would you not agree?"

"You are to marry?" Miss Barrows was incredulous.

"Yes, it will be announced formally this evening, and the banns will be read for the first time this Sunday."

"My brother will be quite disappointed to hear that.

I believe he has a fondness for you. In fact," she pulled a folded piece of paper from her pocket, "he asked me to give this to you. I refused at first. I told him it is not proper and should not be done, but he insisted. And his face looked so sad that I just could not deny him." She pressed the missive into Anne's hand.

"Thank you, but you are right it is not proper." She attempted to give the letter back to Miss Barrows, who refused to take it.

"No, I have done my part. I shall not disappoint my brother by returning home with it."

Anne slipped the note into her pocket. She was curious as to its contents but refused to read it in his sister's presence. Later, she would read it with Richard — preferably after he had been tucked back into bed and possibly even medicated or at least having had a quantity of wine or brandy.

The rest of the stroll about the garden was uneventful. Miss Barrows chattered on about her friends and their accounts of the events of the season and how she longed to join them within a fortnight.

~*~*~*~*~

"You look tired, my dear," Richard whispered as she sat down next to him again. The rest of the gentlemen had wandered off to play a game of croquet with the ladies while Georgiana and Maria played shuttlecock with Mrs.

Ainsley and Mrs. Jenkins. "What did Miss Barrows give you?"

"Were you watching me?" She quite liked the idea that he had been.

"I was. Now, what did she give you?"

Anne drew the folded paper from her pocket and handed it to him. "I am not sure. I just know it is from her brother. I was going to bring it to you later, but since you will not stop until you have your answers, you may have it now. I have not read it."

Richard took the letter and unfolded it. Anne watched his face darken as he read it. "I will kill him," he muttered.

Anne took the letter from him and read.

My dear Miss de Bourgh,

I beg of you to reconsider your response to my proposal. I am in possession of information about your family which, should it fall into the wrong hands, could severely blacken your reputation. I have it on good authority that your mother's marriage was a patched-up affair and that you, in fact, are not Sir Louis' daughter and therefore, not his heir but a clutching and clawing by-blow. Once this information is made known, both you and your mother will, of course, have to leave Rosings and others will have to see to its disposal. I doubt you will be left with very much on which to survive and knowing your delicate constitution, I do fear for your well-being. However, none of that need happen if you will but make me the happiest of men and accept my proposal. I will give you one day to consider your answer. I expect your reply before the moon rises tomorrow, or by morning there will be a very interesting story in the Times. Sincerely,

C.B.

Anne turned pale as she read. Richard drew her as close to his side as his wheeled contraption would allow. Concern that she might faint gripped his heart. "Anne, will you be well? Shall I call for help?" Silently he cursed the leg that kept him from helping her himself.

Anne nodded slowly. "I shall be well." She lifted tear-filled eyes to him. "But I do not know how we can stop him, and his sister knows I have already accepted your proposal. When she goes home and tells him, he will write his false story and have it published. My home...my reputation...my mother's reputation..." A tear slid down her cheek.

Richard cupped her face in his hands and brushed the tear away with his thumb. "He will not harm you," he said firmly before placing a quick kiss on her forehead and releasing her. "Alcock!" he shouted.

The colonel turned and hurried toward him.

"Your men, have they had time to learn anything?"

"I will not know until a bit later today when I ride in to Coburg's. What has happened?"

Richard took the letter from Anne and handed it to his friend.

"No!" said Anne trying to snatch the letter away from Richard.

"Do not worry, my dear. He has already been made aware of the particulars of your mother's arranged marriage. He will not misuse the information. I trust him with my life, and more importantly, I would trust him with yours."

Chapter 13

Adrian Cranfield entered Coburg's and took a seat.

"Can I get you some refreshment, sir?" a slightly rounded older gentleman asked.

"Two pints." Cranfield placed his coins on the table. The gentleman swept them into his hand and raised an eyebrow slightly at the request.

"My nephew will be joining me," explained Cranfield.

"You have relatives near here?" The barkeeper turned from him for a moment. "Nate, two pints," he called across the room. "My son. He's learning to run the place. Does a fine job most days."

"Always wanted a son," commented Cranfield.

"No son? You have daughters then?"

Cranfield shook his head. "Never married. My nephew is the closest I have to a son."

"And he's from 'round here?" Coburg patted his son on the shoulder as the younger man placed three tankards on the table. He grabbed one and slid onto the bench across from Cranfield.

"No, his family hails from the North, but he lives in Town now. He is visiting with friends."

"And who are these friends?"

"One, Miss Bennet, I know only by name and not face though I am here in hopes of remedying that. He seems quite complimentary of her." The two gentlemen shared a chuckle at that.

"Ah, the fancies of youth," murmured Coburg.

"Aye." Cranfield lifted his cup in salute. "I wish him better luck than I." He took a drink of his ale and returned the mug to the table. "The other fellow, Darcy, I know well. A right fine gentleman he is."

"That he is," Coburg agreed. "Comes in to see me every time he visits his aunt." He eyed Cranfield's clothing. "Pardon me for saying so, but you do not appear to be of the same station as Mr. Darcy."

"Aye, that I am not. I am a tradesman through and through. Darcy has blinders on when it comes to class lines as long as a man has integrity and treats him well."

Coburg mumbled his agreement.

Cranfield continued, "I and my sister both wished to see her son established as a gentleman, and Darcy has been assisting him with his search for an estate."

"Ah," Coburg rose from the bench as Darcy and Bingley entered the tavern. "Speaking of the devil," he said with a grin. "I will get another pint. Nice to get to know a bit about those who darken my door." He wiped his hand on his apron and extended it to Cranfield. "Jeremiah Coburg, my son is Nate. If you ever have need of anything, just give us a shout. And your name?"

"Adrian Cranfield. I travel these roads often. I shall have to make a point to rest my horse here."

Mr. Coburg nodded and then greeted Darcy and introduced himself to Bingley.

"I see Coburg has been entertaining you. He is a talkative fellow. One must always spend a few moments informing him of your life before he will leave you to your business," said Darcy. "Have you been waiting long?"

"Just a few minutes. If I had known you were coming, I would have had your beverage waiting for you."

Coburg hustled over with the additional tankard. "Your uncle tells me that Darcy is helping you find an estate."

"He is. I have a lease on one in Hertfordshire, but in all honesty, I have not spent a great deal of time there." Bingley looked quickly at his uncle and then away. "My sister wished to spend the season in town."

"And you hoped to marry her off?" There was a twinkle in the elderly gentleman's eye. "Had more than one sister myself. At a certain age, they become unbearable until they have their eye on a man."

"Not always." Bingley chuckled and darted a look at Darcy. "It can grow worse if the gentleman has no eye for the sister."

165

"Set her cap at Darcy, did she?" Cranfield chuckled. "She has high aspirations at least."

"Aspirations that are about to be dashed." Bingley lifted an eyebrow at his uncle and gave him a meaningful look.

Coburg, who had remained, leaning against the booth, nearly choked on his ale. "Darcy is getting married?"

Darcy grinned from ear to ear. "I am. You may have met her. She was staying with her cousin, the parson."

Coburg looked confused. "Miss Bennet?" His eyes went from Darcy to Cranfield to Bingley and back to Darcy.

"Miss Bennet?" Cranfield repeated as confused as Coburg. "Did you not write me of a Miss Bennet you wished to court?" he asked his nephew.

"Yes," replied Bingley.

Darcy laughed. "It is not the same Miss Bennet. I am to marry Miss Elizabeth Bennet, and Bingley here has his heart set on Miss Jane Bennet, Miss Elizabeth's older sister."

"So you shall be brothers in truth?"

"That is the hope, Uncle."

Coburg shook his head and lowered his voice. "But Darcy, what of your cousin?"

"No need to fear, Mr. Coburg. She is also to be married, just not to me. It seems she is very fond of my cousin, Colonel Fitzwilliam."

"Fitzwilliam and Miss de Bourgh? Well, I never. Congratulations to the lot of you. Mr. Cranfield, it's been a pleasure." He nodded and left to care for a new set of customers who had entered.

Darcy eyed Bingley's uncle, who had suddenly found the contents of his tankard to be worthy of close scrutiny. "I recently learned of an interesting connection between your family and mine."

Cranfield nodded. "Aye, it is interesting. That is one way of saying it."

"It seems I look a lot like you did at my age, Uncle."

Cranfield nodded again. "That you do."

"It nearly gave my aunt an apoplexy when she saw him. As it was, she had to be carried to a couch. It seems the incident could have been avoided."

Cranfield shook his head. "No, it could not have been avoided. I was never to speak of it."

"But you are here now, and you obviously recognize the name." Bingley held his uncle's gaze. "Do you still wish to accept Miss de Bourgh's invitation for dinner?"

"I wish to take a ride." Cranfield placed his empty cup on the table. "I will wait for you outside." He stood quickly and with a wave of thanks to Coburg, exited the building.

He was already mounted when the two younger men exited. "This way." He nodded toward his left and with a pat to his mount's neck and a cluck of his tongue, he was gone. He only slowed when he neared the crest of a hill. It was not on the road; he had swung off the road a few minutes back and crossed some open field. He stopped under a cluster of trees and flicked his reins over a low branch. He patted his horse's nose. Then, he turned and walked a few feet to the top of the crest.

"I have spent many hours in this spot," he explained to Darcy and Bingley, who had joined him. "It was the closest I dare come to seeing her." He nodded toward the manor house in the distance. "I know the land well from all my studying. There," he motioned to his left, "is a new orchard started just seven years ago. And there, that groom, always wears a bit of red somewhere on his person. He just started working for her two years ago. Not much I don't know about the place. And it is why I was glad to have your invitation. There's trouble afoot, but I could not contact anyone. It was part of the agreement." He spat on the ground. "And since your Uncle John's been gone, Darcy, I have had not a word from anyone of her family, but then again, I only heard from John on rare occasions when he thought it safe to contact me."

"So my invitation, or more correctly Miss de Bourgh's invitation, breaks the agreement in a way that is acceptable?"

Cranfield nodded.

"The agreement?" Darcy began. "It was between you and the late Lord Matlock?"

"It was, but not just he is aware of it. There are still a

few who remain and could cause mischief if the terms of the agreement were breached."

"So, even after you learned of the first Lord Matlock's death and then Sir Louis' death, you were bound by this agreement and had no way to safely contact my aunt?"

"Precisely." He turned and looked at Bingley. "I still am not completely certain my acceptance of your invitation will not cause harm. You must know that should those who remain decide to take action against me, any remaining inheritance you were to receive on my death would be gone." He drew a long breath. "My death would not be far into the future and could bring a great deal of shame to you unless you disavow me as a family member. Before I set one foot on de Bourgh's land, you must promise me that you will cut all ties with me should it be necessary."

"I...I am not sure I can make that promise."

"You must, or not only you but your sisters and any chance you might have of happiness with Miss Bennet will be affected. The knowledge that you will endure the same unhappiness I have is not something I wish to ponder for the remainder of my life, fleeting as it might be."

Bingley shook his head, and removing his hat, ran a hand through his hair. "Then, I have no option but to promise."

"Then I will join you for dinner. Lord and Lady Matlock are in attendance?"

"They are." Bingley looked at his uncle in confusion.

"I listen. There are people who talk."

"People you will not tell us about?" asked Darcy.

"Exactly."

"Will you tell us of the trouble you mentioned or the danger you face?"

"It is intricately tied together." Cranfield gave Darcy a guarded look.

"Being well-informed is not always the safest choice."

"So there are those who do not wish for this information you have to be known."

Cranfield nodded and tapped his nose.

Darcy turned so that his back was to Rosings and his face was to Cranfield. "It has something to do with the French and at least part of Rosings' lands?"

Cranfield's eyes narrowed. "What do you know?"

"Not much," said Darcy. "Richard was nearly killed so that he would not be able to court Anne. Then, Anne received a proposal from a gentleman who was very intent upon gaining Rosings and equally as angry at her refusal. The same man was behind the attack upon Richard. And while Richard was lying on the ground after the attack, he heard the men this man had hired talking about a wagon and the French."

"You speak of Barrows?"

Darcy nodded. "I do."

"Will he be at the dinner this evening?"

"No, but his sister may be."

Cranfield cursed. "Then your promise, Nephew, may indeed be called upon." He looked out away from Rosings. "My boats dock near here. As everyone is aware, there are those who profit from the importation of goods which are restricted or prohibited. Some profit from perfectly legal goods transported in such a way as to avoid taxation. My company does not deal in such goods. However, what is truth and what is made to appear as truth are often two very different things."

"They will lie about you?"

"They will not just lie about me. They will make it look like I have betrayed my country. They do not wish to merely have my reputation tarnished; they will make sure I hang."

"Then why attend this dinner?"

Cranfield looked at the ground. "I have been offered a chance to see her," he whispered. He lifted eyes that shimmered with unshed tears to his nephew. "I long to see her one last time and to do what I can to protect her."

"The trouble you mentioned?"

Cranfield nodded. "As you have mentioned, there are those who are most anxious to gain possession of Rosings, but we must leave. We have been here too long already." He nodded to a couple of horsemen, who were off in the distance but decidedly headed toward them. He hurried over to his horse. "It appears my crossing onto deBourgh land will not go unnoticed." He swung up into his saddle.

"Gentlemen, I would appreciate it if you would flank me until we are at the house."

"You think they would shoot you?"

"It would not be the first time." With a last look over his shoulder at the approaching men, he took his place between his nephew and Darcy. "Do you think she will even see me?"

Darcy smiled. "She will see you though she fears you will not wish to see her."

"Why would she think that?"

"What is truth is not always what is made to appear as truth, or some such thing a wise man once told me." Darcy gave Cranfield a wink as he nudged his horse to go faster. "I suggest we speak of it at the house where there is less chance of our conversation being interrupted by gunfire."

Chapter 14

"Cranfield." Lord Matlock clapped the man on the shoulder in a welcoming fashion as he entered the dower house. "A word, if you do not mind." Noting the look of suspicion on the man's face, he added, "A friendly word." He chuckled. "My wife constantly reminds me I need to spend time on small talk and pleasantries. She says neglecting them makes people uneasy."

"She would be right." The right side of Cranfield's mouth curved up into a half smile.

"My apologies." Lord Matlock motioned for Cranfield to enter the room ahead of him before turning to Bingley and Darcy. "I believe you will find your ladies, as well as the rest of the guests, in the garden." Bingley took a step toward the sitting room, but Lord Matlock held up his hand and lowered his voice. "You have nothing to fear, my boy. I have a family apology to make, and I believe a reunion would be better in private."

"Right," agreed Bingley and followed Darcy toward the garden.

Lord Matlock closed the door gently. "My father was wrong."

Cranfield gave a small snort of laughter. "You do not circle a topic, do you?"

Lord Matlock smiled. "I see very little need of fluffing the subject unless I need to convince the other party that my position on a topic is right and theirs is wrong. But, I believe on this fact we are in agreement. What my father and his cohorts did to you and to my sister was wrong — unpardonable really — though I do hope you will not hold his actions against me." Lord Matlock took a seat next to Cranfield. "He received no support from either John or me in this decision, and he only garnered Catherine's cooperation through threat of dire consequences — not even de Bourgh entered the arrangement willingly. As I am sure you are aware, my father could be very persuasive in his arguments." He straightened the sleeves of his jacket, the only sign of his unease with the topic being discussed. "I must ask what his demands were of you. I know there must have been an agreement for you have been quite prosperous in your business."

Cranfield cocked his head to the side and narrowed his eyes. "I am to believe you know naught of his arrangement with me?"

"Whether you believe me or not will make it no less true." Lord Matlock fidgeted with the cuff of his left sleeve. "I ceased communication with my father after he refused to hear my pleas on my sister's behalf. I was never meant to be his heir, and when John died suddenly, many secrets died with him. An agreement as must have existed between you and my father was surely not one which would have been recorded in his important documents and passed down to me. Your dealings were too close to our family. A written record may have fallen into the wrong hands and brought more scandal than even my father would have been able to quell."

Cranfield sighed. "Very well." He rose and paced the room. "I am never to speak her name. I am never to contact her or any of her family. I am allowed to have contact with her family only if they first contact me." He counted off the regulations on his fingers. "I am never to set foot on Matlock or de Bourgh property unless invited. I am never to speak of this arrangement unless granted permission by the Earl of Matlock."

"And if you do not comply?"

"If I break any of these rules, no matter how small the infraction might be, I will be branded a traitor. There are men even now who may be arranging things so that it will look as though I not only transport illegal goods but also provide passage on my ships for those who would support our enemy. It will be made to look as if I am aiding the French."

Matlock let out a slow whistle. "So your penalty would harm not only you but all associated with you."

Cranfield nodded. "Your father knew that to threaten to do harm only to me would not have been effective. He tried."

Lord Matlock closed his eyes and grimaced. "What did he do to you?"

Cranfield removed his jacket and his waistcoat. "I prefer to show you a portion." He lifted his shirt. White raised scars streaked across his back and a knotted white patch of skin stood out against his side. H pointed to his side. "My leg has another scar similar to this."

For a few moments, Lord Matlock could not do more than stare at Cranfield in horror. "You were beaten?" he finally managed to ask.

"Flogged might be a more accurate term, my lord— a lash for every refusal" Cranfield tucked his shirt back into his breeches. "Since I still refused one term of my agreement no matter the number of lashes, I was given the opportunity to fight to retain the right to say her name. Wielding a sword after such a beating is not an easy task and the scar on my side and a matching one on my leg and a smaller slash on my arm are from that battle. I did not win."

"You dueled for the right to say her name?" Matlock shook his head in disbelief.

"I did. I believe your father was afraid I might use that right to somehow circumvent the other restrictions, and I am certain he would have been correct in that assumption. I love your sister with a love that will only die when I do, my lord." He buttoned his waistcoat. "To ensure I did not cause issue with the nuptials, I was held in a cell not far from here. My wounds would have festered and a fever would have surely killed me in that place had it not been for one kind servant. I, to this day, do not know how he came to tend me, but I am grateful to whoever sent him."

"What do you mean when you say you were held in a cell not far from here?"

"At the far end of the property, there are at least two underground rooms. Their use, I believe, was normally for noble purposes." He sat once again and lowered his voice. "Purposes known to the crown and overseen, in part, by your father. Your father was not all bad, my lord. He actively aided those seeking refuge on English soil."

There was a knock at the door.

"Come," called Lord Matlock.

"My lord," said Kellet entering the room with a tea tray. "Miss de Bourgh insists that you offer Mr. Cranfield some refreshment." He placed the tray on the table, keeping his face to Lord Matlock.

"It is you!" Cranfield leapt from his chair and turned the elderly butler so that he could see his face. "It is." He touched the man's face as if he did not believe what he was seeing. "It really is you. You are the one who saved me by tending to my wounds."

"Is this true?" asked Lord Matlock.

Kellet swallowed audibly and looked at the floor. "It is, my lord."

"Tell me," said Cranfield. "Who sent you to tend to me?"

"My lord?" Kellet looked at Lord Matlock for permission.

"I am as curious as Mr. Cranfield. Please tell us."

"So I shall not be sent packing?" He shifted uneasily, looking toward the door as if wishing for an escape.

"No. Why would you be sacked?"

"When I was sent, I was instructed that should Lady Catherine's family ever learn of my part in helping Mr. Cranfield, I would be dismissed without reference or pay."

"I can assure you that you shall still have employment at Rosings," said Lord Matlock. "Now, please tell us."

"Very well, my lord. It was my master who sent me."

"De Bourgh?" Matlock's brows rose high in astonishment.

"Yes, my lord."

"Why?" said Cranfield. "Why would de Bourgh help me?"

"You were injured, sir." The look on Kellet's face let both men know that there was more he was not saying.

"Mr. Kellet," began Lord Matlock. "I am not my father."

"I understand that, my lord. You are, in my opinion, much better than he."

Lord Matlock chuckled. "You dare to share your opinion but not the information we seek?"

"I spoke of it once when questioned, my lord, and the man died not long after. I do not wish to see that happen to you."

"Indeed? And who was this man?"

"Your brother, my lord."

"John?"

"Yes, my lord."

"And you fear I shall meet a similar fate if you tell me about it?"

"I do, my lord."

"Then tell me," said Cranfield. "I am already in danger of a similar fate."

"After all I have heard this evening, we are all likely in danger just from Cranfield's presence," said Lord Matlock. "And, if there is danger to be faced, would it not be better to face that danger with all the facts possible?"

"It may be," said Kellet.

"Then you have my permission to tell me all you know. I am aware of the risk it may pose to my safety." Lord Matlock motioned to a chair.

"Very well, my lord. My master was my master for many years. He brought me to England with him when he came. I owed him much for his protection and was willing to do whatever he asked." He took a seat at Lord Matlock's insistence. "I was not the only person he brought to England. Along with the people, he also brought information for which he received the king's reward in the form of Rosings."

Lord Matlock's eyes grew wide. "De Bourgh was an informant?"

"Yes, my lord. He wished to insure his safe arrival and plead for help for his family who remained in France."

"He was of noble birth, was he not?"

"He was, my lord."

"Why did his family not travel with him?" asked Cranfield.

"Most of them did, but his sister's husband did not believe there was reason to flee. A year later when the unrest had not ceased but seemed to be increasing, Madame Henault was able to convince her husband to leave. They were granted safe passage, which was provided by your father, my lord."

Lord Matlock closed his eyes and nodded his head as if finally understanding something. "Passage which was provided in exchange for de Bourgh marrying my sister and putting to rest a possible scandal — a favour for a favour."

"And a connection to the land," added Cranfield. "The rooms were important to the safe arrival of many, those seeking safety and those who were providing valuable information. Are they still a valuable asset?"

Kellet nodded.

Lord Matlock's brows drew together in question.

"I assume your father had many connections within the government who brought him power," said Cranfield. "Who would have been an asset politically? Someone who knew of the operations on this land and wished to keep them from being known?"

"It would be a good reason to seek a connection to the land." Matlock scrubbed his face with his hands. "I fear you are wrong, Cranfield. My father may have done what appeared to be good, but I am certain it was done only for his own benefit and no one else's."

The three men had sat in silence for a few moments before Kellet rose to leave.

"Mr. Kellet," Lord Matlock called to him. "John was killed in an accident. Why do you think it came as a result of your conversation with him?"

Kellet's face turned ashen. "My lord, I dare not say."

Cranfield stood and walked to the window. "Not all the hidden activity happening on this land is legal, and your father knew of it, my lord, but your brother did not." He turned to face the room. "Why else would your father be able to threaten me with being marked a traitor if he did not have access to items which would make the claim believable."

"But he could create documents which if found on your vessels would be damning."

Cranfield nodded. "True, but I know what I heard when he uttered the threat, my lord. He knew." He walked closer to Kellet. "Your master. When did he learn of how his land was being used?"

"Two months before his death." Kellet attempted to school his features into implacability but the glistening of his eyes and his lowered gaze told of both his grief and discomfort in speaking of Sir Louis' death.

"He was a good man," said Cranfield. "I know. I listened. It was reassuring to know that she was not tied to some reprobate." He laid a hand on the butler's shoulder. "His death was not as reported, was it?"

Kellet's jaw clenched in an effort to keep control of his emotions. "No," he finally managed.

"It was not that the fever following his accident had damaged his heart?" asked Lord Matlock.

"If the report said it was his heart, then I expect it was his heart," said Cranfield. "However, I suspect his heart would have survived many more years if it had not been helped along the path of destruction. And I very much suspect his accident was not an accident."

"Poison?" Lord Matlock's shook his head as if the concept was impossible to believe. "Who would do such a thing?"

"Whoever had the most to lose should the information fall into the wrong hands."

"My father?" Matlock fell back in his chair, eyes wide and mouth open in shock.

Cranfield shook his head. "No, your father would have

himself protected well enough to not be included in any activity on which the crown might frown. My guess would be Barrows. His land abuts Rosings, and he needs support to retain his seat in parliament."

"Mrs. Barrows." Kellet barely spoke above a whisper. "She was here far more often than her husband."

There was a series of three soft knocks at the door. Kellet looked nervously from the door to Lord Matlock.

"My wife," he said, "and I would assume my sister." He rose and straightened his jacket. "I will speak to them in the hall." He paused before leaving the room and turned to Cranfield. "You have always had my approval."

Cranfield stared at the door after it closed behind Lord Matlock. He tugged at his cravat and tried to breathe deeply to steady his nerves. His heart beat a rapid rhythm. He shifted from foot to foot. He sat down only to stand again. Finally, the door opened, and there she was, standing beside her brother.

Lord Matlock gave her a small nudge to enter the room. "If you need me, I will be out here for the next half hour, after which time I will rejoin you along with my wife, niece and son." He gave Catherine one more nudge and closed the door softly behind her.

It was silent in the room for a few minutes before Cranfield laughed nervously. "I have dreamt of the day I should see you again, but in all my dreaming I never once considered a proper greeting." He stepped toward her. "I could say it is good to see you, and it would be true, or I could say I missed you, for I did so very much." He shook his head and stepped closer. "But those greetings do not begin to convey my joy at this moment — a moment I never thought would happen, but the hope of which has kept me alive all these years." He took her hand and brought it to his lips.

She reached up and placed a hand on his cheek. "You do know it was not my choice to marry?"

He nodded. "And you must know I would have stopped it if I were able."

"And you never contacted me because you were prevented?"

"Ah, my love, I could never have stayed away from you willingly." He kissed her hand once again before pulling her into his embrace. "Please do not ask me to leave you, for I do not have the strength to be separated from you again."

She pulled back slightly to look up at him. "Never. I would never ask you to leave." A smile lit her face despite the tears which flowed down her cheeks. "Adrian?" She reached up to touch his cheek once again. "Kiss me." She placed a finger on his lips as he lowered his head to do as she had asked. "But first say my name as you used to."

"Ah, Kate," he whispered against her lips before claiming them with all the sweetness and passion he had been denied for so long.

Chapter 15

Mrs. Barrows froze as she entered the room. The greeting she was about to make died on her lips as her eyes landed on Bingley.

"I hear he looks a lot like his uncle," said Anne as she took Mrs. Barrows' hand in greeting.

Mrs. Barrows snapped her mouth closed and blinked at Anne.

"My mother says he looks a lot like his uncle," prodded Anne.

"Indeed he does," replied Mrs. Barrows. Her eyes narrowed a bit. "Surely your mother is not allowing you to associate with people of a lower station. It is most unseemly." She looked to her daughter, who was conversing with Jane and Bingley. "Abigail," she called in a stern tone. "We are expecting guests this evening, and your brother's business took longer than expected. You need to come away now."

"We are also having guests at our meal tonight."

Mrs. Barrows gave a derisive snort. "Of course you are, my dear; this is a house party after all."

Anne smiled a small tight smile, the one she used when her mother said something demeaning. "You mistake my meaning, Mrs. Barrows. I meant that we have an additional guest this evening. Mr. Bingley's uncle has accepted my invitation to join us."

Mrs. Barrows' eyebrows rose in surprise. "Cranfield is here?"

"He is." Mrs. Barrows jumped at the sound of Lord Matlock's voice. "With my blessing," he added in a tone that held a warning.

"Of course, my lord," said Mrs. Barrows as her daughter joined her. "It is a pity we have prior arrangements and are unable to attend tonight's dinner." The look of disgust on her face gave lie to the sweetness of her voice.

"I am sure it is," said Lord Matlock. "Might I walk you to the door?"

"That is very gracious of you, my lord, but I do not require special treatment."

"Oh, but I believe you do," said Lord Matlock. "Besides, I have sent Kellet to tend to something, and that would leave you to open the door on your own. We cannot be so uncivilized as to allow that, can we?"

"Surely a footman could see to the door."

"They are all attending to duties. I am afraid you are

left only with my escort at present." He smiled and, extending an arm to each lady, led them from the room.

~*~*~*~*~*~

"The audacity of some people!" Mrs. Barrows huffed as she took her seat in the carriage and arranged her skirts. "Ushering us out as if we were unwanted while a tradesman's son sits comfortably in the drawing room."

"Oh, but Mama, Mr. Bingley will soon own an estate. He has already been leasing one, and he is the most pleasant fellow." Miss Barrows smoothed her skirt.

"He is a tradesman's son and, as such, he is beneath you. I would prefer if you not spend time associating with the likes of him." Her mother's voice was firm.

"Indeed," agreed her brother, who sat on the opposing bench. "He is beneath us. He'll not be welcomed to Rosings again once I marry Miss de Bourgh. Class lines must be strictly observed, or society will be in shambles." He tapped her knee with his walking stick. "Did you give Miss de Bourgh my letter?"

"I did, and it was the strangest thing. She tucked it into her pocket, and when our walk was through, she gave it to Colonel Fitzwilliam to read." She tilted her head and pursed her lips. "I suppose he may require such things of her since they are to be wed. I should not like to have such a heavy-handed man as my intended, much less my husband." She shrugged. "Papa would not allow such a man to claim me." She settled back in her seat satisfied with her conclusion.

"Miss de Bourgh is to marry Colonel Fitzwilliam?" asked her mother in surprise.

"Three weeks hence. I believe the first of the banns will be called this Sunday."

She lifted a brow and gave her son a knowing look. "It may be, unless she decides to call it off. These things happen, you know."

"Oh, Mama. She is quite in love with him, and he with her. I am quite certain there will be a wedding. And the wedding breakfast...oh, we must attend!"

Her mother patted her arm. "You will be in London, taking rides in the park and dancing with fine gentlemen. You will be far too busy to take time away for a wedding breakfast."

"Do you think so? I am quite excited to have my season, even if it is only a small one." Her raptures about her dresses and the parties she would attend as well as her friends, who were awaiting her arrival and who had sent the most interesting letters, filled the remainder of the ride.

"I would like to take a small turn in the garden, Christopher," said her mother as she alighted from the carriage. They walked together in silence until they reached the rose garden. "Will you still give her until tomorrow evening?"

"I think I must."

"Rosings is not lost until she is wed. There is still time. Rumours can be started, and accidents can happen — one must not wed while in mourning." She noted the look of surprise on her son's face and patted his arm. "Accidents can be fatal."

They walked on once again in silence for a time. "I understand Mr. Bingley's uncle has joined the house party."

"And why do I need to know this?"

"You do remember the story I told you about Lady Catherine's marriage?" He nodded, and she continued, "Mr. Bingley's uncle is Adrian Cranfield."

His eyes grew wide. "The Cranfield?"

"One and the same. He knows far too much about our business, and he may have already shared his knowledge with the others in attendance. I fear it is the reason Lord Matlock escorted me to the door." She led him to a bench and took a seat. "It could pose a challenging issue to overcome, but I do not believe as of yet it is insurmountable. However, we must act quickly."

"What are we to do?"

She shrugged, "We have options."

"Such as?"

"You have an article that will taint the de Bourgh name, and I have a letter that appears to be in his hand claiming you as his son, leaving you the rightful heir of

Rosings. However, you may need to take me in as I am sure your father will cast me out when he hears of the supposed indiscretion."

"I do not like that option. Tell me another."

"Very well. Again we submit the anonymous article making sure to hint at Cranfield being Anne's father. There are documents that can be found on one of his ships that would make him appear disloyal to the crown. Anne will not only be illegitimate but also the daughter of a traitor. Neither she nor her mother will recover from such a blow." She gave him a small smile. "It is not as if either would have survived long after your marriage anyway, would they?"

Mr. Barrows chuckled. "Are these the only options? There is still Matlock, who could wield some power and ruin either of those plans."

"Yes, I had thought of that." She looked around the garden as if taking in the beauty of the night. "Fires are known to start accidentally." She paused to allow time for him to process what she had suggested. "However, you would need to oversee such a task personally much as I saw to Sir Louis' inability to recover from his accident."

Mr. Barrows stood and strode about the bench in a circle. Finally, he came to a stop. "Matlock is staying at Rosings with Lady Catherine. We cannot put a torch to both. It would be too conspicuous, and I would be left in need of a residence."

"Easily solved, my son. A cry will go out about the fire — preferably not until it is beyond dousing. Lord Matlock and Lady Catherine will, of course, rush to the dower house. A loosened wheel or a startled horse may cause an issue, and with everyone focused on the fire, they will not be looked for until it is far too late to help them."

~*~*~*~*~*~

Richard pulled himself to a sitting position. Sleep, it seemed, was determined to elude him tonight. He shoved another pillow behind his back and settled back, longing for a book to read, but dragging himself across the bed to light a candle seemed a ridiculous task since he had already finished both books that lay on his night stand. So instead, his thoughts turned to the events of the day.

After dinner had concluded, while the rest of the occupants of the house adjourned to the sitting room to play cards, he had been required to remain behind and listen to the details his father had learned about Cranfield. It still seemed incredible that one of his own relations had treated someone as Cranfield had been treated. And to learn that Anne was correct in assuming her father's accident was not an accident made him very thankful to have been of less interest than a wagon of French goods to the men who had startled his horse.

Tomorrow, they must take action to prevent anything further from happening. He was certain that Mrs. Barrows, knowing that Cranfield was in residence, would find some way to cause trouble. That man had been through enough. He deserved to finally find his happiness, and his aunt appeared more than willing to help him find it. He chuckled softly to himself. He had never expected to see Aunt Catherine so enamoured with anyone, let alone a tradesmen, but she was still clearly besotted even though twenty-five years had passed. The thought of it made him smile and consider his happy future. He leaned his head back and closed his eyes. Perhaps with these happy thoughts, his mind would finally allow him the rest his body craved.

Sleep was just creeping upon him when its progression was halted by the sound of glass breaking somewhere below him. He sat still, even his breathing stopped as he strained to hear any further sounds. Somewhere outside his window that was just slightly ajar, he heard the sounds of feet moving away at a quick pace. He pulled himself to the edge of his bed and using the bed, then the night stand, and finally the wall for support, hopped his way to the window, knowing full well the effort would probably prove pointless as the darkness of the night would surely hide any figures. Still he pulled aside the curtain and looked out to see two figures fleeing in the direction of the road. He blinked, startled that he was able to see them so well and at such a distance at this hour of the night. He looked toward the sky, perhaps it was a full moon, and he had forgotten. Seeing the moon was no larger than a sliver of light, he looked around searching for the source of illumination. The foggy grasp of sleep seemed to still have a hold on him until he smelt it. The smoke that blew into his room on the night breeze brought him fully to his senses. Peering down, he could see the glow of orange and yellows from the lower level of the dower house. His bare foot could now feel the warmth radiating through the floor.

"Fire!" he yelled to the emptiness of his room as he hopped toward the door. The others must be roused. He stopped his progression as his hand brushed against the bell pull. He rang it three times in rapid succession before continuing to the door. He threw the door open, nearly knocking himself down in the process. "Fire!" he yelled again. "Fire!" The door across from his pulled open slowly. "Darcy, fire! We must get everyone out! Quickly before it consumes the stairs. The flames are beneath my room." He hopped down the hall, banging on doors as he went and yelling to the occupants.

A servant came running toward him. "Go back, rouse the others and get out," he cried. Dutifully, the servant did as instructed. "Gather in the garden so we can account for everyone." He called after the servant and to those making their way down the stairs. He leaned against the wall as he watched everyone descend the stairs except Darcy.

"That is everyone. We can go now." Darcy draped Richard's arm around his shoulders. "Lean into me and use the other hand on the balustrade if you can."

Halfway down, Richard leaned more heavily into Darcy as he pulled his robe to cover his mouth and nose. The thick smoke stung his eyes and burned his throat. As they reached the bottom of the staircase, he pushed Darcy away. "Let go of me," he said as he sank onto the step. Reaching up, he grabbed Darcy and pulled him to sit beside him. "The layer of smoke looks to be less thick here." He then slid onto the floor and began pulling himself along toward the garden door and away from the fire.

He coughed and gasped for air as he finally pulled himself out into the garden. In a moment, there were footmen on either side of him, hoisting him onto his good leg and assisting him to where the others had gathered.

"We are all here, save one," said Bingley. "I have sent a runner to Rosings to fetch more buckets and men. The others have formed a line to the stream and the buckets are being filled."

"Are there any injuries?"

"None. Your call was early; the way was still clear."

"And the one who is missing? Who is that?"

"Mr. Kellet."

Chapter 16

Frustration settled in firmly around Richard as he watched the efforts to fight the fire. He longed to be useful, but with only one good leg, he was useless. His frustration only eased slightly as he saw help from Rosings arrive.

As the first rays of morning crested the horizon, there were shouts of victory as the fire was finally reduced to a few smouldering embers. Soon the damage could be more easily seen. Darcy came to help him from the bench and into the house to assess the damages. The study below his room and everything to the front of it and above it were gone. The stairs they had taken to safety stood, but just barely. The doors to the rooms across the hall from the study were charred but not gone. The smell of smoke was thick in the air, and black sooty water ran underfoot everywhere. A few footmen sat in the garden, coughing and gulping in mouthfuls of air. Others wandered about the ruins, shaking their heads and marvelling at the destruction as he did.

Richard and Darcy stood in the middle of what was

once the study. What appeared to be a bottle was molten to the floor near where the window used to be, a rock lay next to it. Richard pointed to it. "I heard glass breaking. It is what roused me from my bed."

"So a deliberate fire?" asked Darcy.

Richard nodded. "I also saw figures running toward the road. I have been wishing to investigate but this leg…"

"We will send out a party of men." Darcy gave his cousin a sideward glance. "And perhaps the curricle could be made available for your use?"

Richard sighed in relief. "Thank you, Darcy. It has been a trial being confined to that blasted bench."

Darcy laughed. "I have no doubt of that."

"Have you seen my father?"

Darcy shook his head. "No."

"John," Richard called to the groomsman who had first come upon him after his accident, "did Lord Matlock and Lady Catherine accompany the party from Rosings?"

"Yes, sir. I saddled horses for them before I left."

"They rode?"

"Yes, sir, I assume they did, but I left before seeing them depart. My duty was to see their horses ready."

"Have you seen them or their horses?"

"I have not, sir."

Richard felt Darcy's grasp tighten on his waist, and he knew he was not the only one whose mind ran rampant with various and unpleasant scenarios for why they had not arrived. "Would you be so kind as to prepare the curricle for me?"

John smiled and bowed. "Right away, sir. And your horse, Mr. Darcy, would you like him readied?"

"I would, thank you." The groomsman bowed once more and hurried away.

Less than half an hour later, Richard sat in the curricle, Anne at his side and insistent on driving. Richard had protested, but, seeing the determined look in her eye, he soon acquiesced. His displeasure faded completely as she smiled at him and placed a kiss on his cheek. They travelled the road toward Rosings but found nothing amiss save an area of bent and matted grass. It was an area he and Darcy agreed that would require further inspection after they had located Lord Matlock and Lady Catherine.

"There are horses in front of the house," said Darcy, who had ridden ahead and circled back to tell them.

"Please, Anne," said Richard, "just a bit faster."

She narrowed her eyes at him. "I'll not be the cause of further damage to your leg. I wish for a husband who can stand before Mr. Collins in three weeks time." Still she clucked to the horse and their pace increased.

Richard slipped an arm about her waist and pulled her a bit closer. "Standing up with you is sufficient encouragement to be careful." He gave her a slight squeeze.

She reined the horse in as she approached the front of Rosings. Darcy stood waiting to help her in securing the horse. She tossed him the ribbons and waited for him to assist first her and then Richard from the curricle.

Lady Catherine pulled the heavy door open as they approached the steps. She rushed out and grabbed Anne, wrapping her in an embrace. "Oh, I am so glad to see you well. I was so afraid…" her voice faded and a sob shook her body.

"I am well, Mother." Anne held her close. "Everyone is well."

"Not everyone," said Lady Catherine, releasing Anne and drying her eyes. "Come. He yet lives."

Anne grabbed her mother by the arm. "Who, Mama?" Images of her uncle passed before her.

"Mr. Kellet," said her mother, leading them into the house and toward the drawing room. "We found him on the road and brought him here to tend. He has been weak and his speech is most incoherent."

"Was he lying beside the road," asked Richard remembering the patch of matted grass.

"He was. It was most horrific, I can assure you. I have not seen a man with such an injury. The blood…" she shook her head at the remembrance, "there was so much of it."

She opened the door to the drawing room slowly. "We have staunched the bleeding and tended to his fever as best we can. We would have taken him to a room with a bed, but it was all I could do to assist your uncle in getting him situated here. I could not have managed the stairs."

Anne moved to stand near where Mr. Kellet lay on a couch. Tears filled her eyes as she looked at the man who had seen to her every need for so many years. True, he was a servant, but to her, he felt more a part of her family than that. She knelt beside him and gently stroked his cheek. "The fire is out," she said. The corner of his mouth curved upward slightly. "The study and the rooms forward of it and above it are destroyed, but the rest remains standing." She smoothed the hair off his forehead. "Everyone made it out. There were no ..." her voice caught, and she inhaled slowly. "There were no injuries. A few will need to recover from breathing too much smoke, but all shall be well." A tear slipped down her cheek, and she let it fall.

"Bar...Bar...rows." The sound was barely a whisper.

"Is he the man you chased?" asked Richard. "I saw two men running toward the road before the fire began. It was you chasing Barrows?" He waited as the man took a few laboured breaths before responding with a yes. "He set the fire?" Kellet moved his head slightly from side to side. "He had help." The statement gained a positive response.

Lord Matlock approached Richard. He held a knife wrapped in a handkerchief. "This is what was used to injure Mr. Kellet. Note the engraving." He held it so that Richard could see where the initials C.B. were etched into the handle.

Richard smiled at Mr. Kellet. "So you caught him." Again the corner of the man's mouth curved up slightly. "I do hope he did not get away unscathed."

"I suspect from what Mr. Kellet has been able to tell me, the man may be lying somewhere in the woods unless his friends found him and carried him off." He placed the knife on a table. "I will send out a party to search as soon as the servants return from the dower house."

"No need," said Darcy. "Before we left the dower house, we sent some out to search for signs of the two men Richard saw running from the house." He stepped closer to his uncle. "Shall I ride for the surgeon?"

Lord Matlock nodded toward the door, and Darcy followed him out of the room. "I fear it will be a fool's errand, but I would like to provide him every hope of recovery and comfort. I would have gone myself upon first finding him, but I could not leave Catherine alone and with everyone else at the dower house…" He shrugged.

Darcy placed a hand on his shoulder. "You had few options. I believe you chose correctly."

His uncle nodded. "Thank you."

"Now, I would like to have a report of his injuries to give to the surgeon, so he can be adequately prepared. I noted the wrapping on his upper arm and hand. Where are the others?"

"Three gashes on his abdomen. One is deeper than the rest, but none was enough to spill more than his blood.

His breathing is laboured, and a fever seems to have set in."

"I will ride as fast as I can," Darcy assured his uncle as he moved toward the door.

~*~*~*~*~*~

The hours of the morning ticked past. Servants began to return. Household tasks were taken up, but a somber air settled over the house. Mrs. Kellet gave instructions to the maids and cook before taking her place next to her brother, who had been moved to his own chamber. Baths were drawn; personal belongings arrived in trunks and were put away in rooms. The surgeon came, cleaned and sutured the wounds, and left medicine and instructions for care.

Richard sat in the drawing room, scowling.

"What causes such a look?" Anne sat down on the settee next to him.

"There are things to be done, and I am confined to this seat or my bed." He expelled a huff of frustration. "I do not like it."

She gave him a sympathetic smile. "I suppose crutches would be acceptable for you to use since the bath chair has been destroyed, but I cannot send anyone to search for them at present. Things are still in a bit of an upheaval, and we are all tired." She laid her head against his shoulder. "Do try to be patient." Her fingers intertwined with his where they lay between them. "Have the men returned from their search?"

He nodded. "Barrows expired some distance into the grove. He appeared to be coming to Rosings though I have not yet figured out why."

She looked up at him. "How did he die?"

He looked at her for a few moments. He knew that while she may tire more readily than most, she was by no stretch of imagination weak. He also knew that she would have her explanation whether she got it from him or some other person. "It appears Mr. Kellet was able to get in a few good slashes of his own. Barrows fell and bled to death."

"Mr. Kellet had a knife?"

He shrugged, jostling her head slightly. He reached across to hold it against him and gave her an apologetic smile. "None was found. I assume Mr. Kellet must have used Barrows' own knife against him."

"Has Mr. Kellet been told of Barrows' death?"

Richard's brows furrowed. "I do not think so."

"He should be told." She began tracing circles on the back of his hand with her free one. "He might rest easier if he knew." She drew in a deep, shaky breath. After a few moments of silence, she continued, "He made a promise to my father…" She drew in another shaky breath and shook her head.

"To protect you and your mother." Richard kissed the top of her head. "And he has done well. You are right; he should be told." He kissed her hair again. "I will tell him as soon as we receive word about Father's meeting with Mr. and Mrs. Barrows. Would you like to accompany me to speak with him?" She sniffled and nodded. "Then you shall." He squeezed her hand and lifted it to his lips. "For now, you must rest."

They lapsed into contented silence. Soon, Richard heard her breathing become soft and even, and her fingers relaxed their grip on his. He returned to watching the activities taking place outside the drawing room window until his father entered.

"You are looking contented for a man confined to the house." Lord Matlock drew a chair close to where his son sat.

"I feel content."

"As you should." He spoke softly so as not to disturb Anne's sleep. "The right woman has a settling effect on a man. I was much like you, you know — a second son, given to strategy, planning and action, eager to take on the next great adventure — until I met your mother. It is as it should be." He patted his son on the shoulder. "Now, we have come to an arrangement of sorts with Barrows." He sighed and shook his head.

"The man had not an inkling of his wife's and son's activities. I feel sorry for the fellow." He stared out the window for a moment. "He has an estate his eldest son has been overseeing in Scotland...a remote piece of land but profitable. It has been decided that he and his wife shall retire there and his son shall take over here. The lad is good from all accounts, but he will be watched. Miss Barrows will be placed in her brother's care until such time as she finds a husband and her care is transferred." He sighed again, the sound of a great weight settling in around him.

"It is not right that the children should suffer for the sins of their parents, be it mother or father." He gave Richard a sad smile. "To punish Mrs. Barrows as would be well within our rights, both for treason and murder, would expose many innocents to censure — our family included. It could also expose some workings that the government would rather keep quiet."

"Will she not still be in a position to do harm while she remains on English soil?"

He shook his head. "It has been made very clear to her by certain officials who met with us that if she crosses them, she will meet with an untimely and unpleasant end. She will remain ensconced in Scotland for the remainder of her days. No travel will be allowed. It is either confinement on her husband's estate or transportation. She has chosen her husband's estate." He lowered his voice a bit more. "I would not be surprised to hear of her passing. The men we spoke with did not seem to be the most forgiving sort of fellows." He straightened his waistcoat.

"They leave within the week. Cranfield has kindly offered passage on one of his ships, and an escort to ensure her arrival in Scotland will be provided. It appears Rosings is safely in Anne's possession once again. I would not be surprised if you were not visited by the men we spoke with today. They were quite pleased to hear the estate would be under the care of a military man."

Richard raised his eyebrows. "I am selling out, Father. I am no longer a military man."

His father chuckled. "I also sold out when the earldom passed to me, but I will assure you, I am still a military man just as you will be. It is in our fibers."

Anne stirred next to him, bringing to mind his promise to her. "Anne wishes to inform Mr. Kellet of the fates of Mrs. Barrows and her son. She thinks he will rest more easily if he knows she and her mother are safe. Would you help me get to his room?"

He stood. "Of course, my son. I must first find your mother and assure her of my safe return and tell her what Catherine needs to know about her friend. Afterwards, I shall return to escort you."

An hour later, Richard sat next to Mr. Kellet's bed, telling the man of Barrows' death and his mother's imminent exile. Anne stood at his side; his father waited a distance away to help him when he was through.

When Richard had arrived at the man's bedside, he had not been sure if Mr. Kellet would hear or understand what was being said, for he lay with his eyes closed. But, as Richard spoke, the corners of Mr. Kellet's mouth curved up, and the lines in his face softened. His breathing slowed and became shallow. His eyes opened for a moment to look at Anne and then Richard. He lifted his hand, and Anne took it. Giving it a faint squeeze and managing a small smile, he closed his eyes once more.

Anne turned away to hide her tears as Richard leaned forward and said softly, near Mr. Kellet's ear. "You've served well. Sir Louis would be satisfied. I can take over from here." Mr. Kellet took one last shallow breath, and Richard pulled Anne onto his lap where he held her while she wept.

Chapter 17

"Did you see to their planting?" Anne lifted a cheek to receive her morning kiss. She motioned to a footman who began gathering a plate of food for Richard as he lowered himself into the seat beside her.

"I did." Darcy placed a cup of coffee in front of his cousin before pouring one for himself. "Richard barked orders, and I ensured they were carried out." They had set out early that morning to the site where Mr. Kellet had been laid to rest one week earlier to plant a few flowers — ones he had particularly admired in her garden now also grew near his headstone.

"Good. I am glad." She sipped her tea. "Mr. Cranfield arrives today." Cranfield had stayed with them for only a few days after the fire. He had business that needed his attention, but he had promised to stay on his return trip. She expected a happy announcement from that quarter before he left again.

"You look happy, my dear."

She patted Richard's hand. "I am content."

"Not happy?" asked Darcy.

She furrowed her brows as she considered how to explain her feelings. "It is hard to feel gladness when you have so recently lost much, but I do not feel despair either. Sadness, I will own, but it lessens as acceptance of change grows." She shrugged. "My heart is content to feel each emotion as it passes. It neither wallows nor flutters. I suppose one could say I was happy if meaning at peace." Her eyes widened. "I do not ever remember feeling as I do now. Mother and Father were never content, you know." She glanced at Darcy. "And then there were Mother's expectations."

"He would have spoken sooner had he known you were uneasy," said Richard before Darcy could apologise.

She blushed. "I do not blame him. I remember begging him not to speak. I foolishly hoped Mother would see reason or give up hope, and I secretly feared she would select someone…" Her blush deepened.

"Far worse?" asked Darcy dryly.

"Yes," she said making Darcy's brows rise. "You did not love me, and I did not love you, but at least I knew you would treat me well and were not after my money. A loveless marriage is bad enough, but one, where I would be treated as nothing or less, would be worse."

Darcy nodded once. "I agree. The first would be bad — the second far worse."

"But neither of us needs fear such an outcome now."

Darcy grinned at her with a twinkle in his eye. "I heard your intended was not only in want of a wife but also an estate."

"Darcy," Richard growled.

"Oh, hush," said Anne with a laugh. "I am quite happy with my intended no matter his fortune." She leaned closer to Darcy and whispered loudly. "He is the son of an earl, you know."

Both men joined her in laughter.

"Ah, it is good to hear laughter around here." Lord Matlock gave Anne a kiss and clapped both Darcy and Richard on the shoulder. "Wanted to deliver the special licenses myself and see to the signing of the marriage contracts." He placed a packet of papers on the table.

"Licenses?" asked Darcy.

Lord Matlock smiled. "A gift for Catherine if she wishes to use it." He winked at Anne. "Perhaps you could instruct her in the proper way to secure a husband." He chuckled at her blush and his son's scowl. "I should like to meet with you and Darcy, Richard, to go over the particulars of the agreement. Anne, you are welcome to join us."

"I should like that, but might I ask that Mother also be allowed to hear the particulars."

"If you wish, my dear." Lord Matlock took the coffee Darcy offered and waved the footmen from the room. "Have you settled on Harrison as a replacement for Kellet?"

"He comes highly recommended by Mrs. Kellet, and he knows the responsibilities of the job. He has been reliable thus far."

Matlock smiled. "He is who I would have chosen. Well done." He tipped his head to the side. "Not so different from filling the ranks of a regiment, is it? Listen to reports, watch behaviours, and assign men according to their skills. There is much you have learned as a colonel that will transfer to master."

"Speaking of colonels," said Richard. "I was visited by two."

"Have they informed you of their operations?"

"They have. It is another reason Harrison seems a good choice. He is not unfamiliar with that particular area of Rosings, and he has their approval."

"Good. It is a sticky business there. Best to keep on the proper side of things." Lord Matlock set his cup on the table. "I shall see all of you in the study in one half hour."

~*~*~*~*~

Anne stood on the terrace overlooking the garden. She breathed deeply of the fresh night air that carried the fragances from the blossoms below her. She blew out her breath, thankful for this moment of quiet. It had been a busy day. It began with the details of her wedding contract and progressed to choosing fabrics and patterns and being measured and draped as the modiste and her helpers, who had accompanied Lady Matlock from town, began work on her trousseau. Even now she knew that details regarding food and beverages for the wedding breakfast were being discussed.

"Are you well?" Richard wrapped one arm around Anne's waist and pulled her back against him.

"I am." She leaned back into him lightly.

"I'll not break or topple, Anne," he whispered in her ear.

"But your leg..."

"Is healing as it should. I have been a very good patient...a task which has not been easy, I assure you."

She laughed. "I have seen you scowl. I know it has tried your patience." She leaned back a bit more and tilted her head up to look at him. "Thank you. I know you do it for me."

"I would do most anything for you."

"You always have," said Anne. "I have been thinking about this lately. Darcy would often question when I asked for assistance, but you would do whatever I asked without a moment's hesitation. If it made me happy, it was done — even if it put you at risk of getting into trouble. You only ever refused if you thought it would do me harm."

"But it is his nature to question."

She turned to face him. "Yes, but it is your nature, as well. You always questioned him. You were not so willing to bear your father's wrath for him."

"But he was a boy."

She smiled at him. "Perhaps." Her arms wound around his neck. "Or perhaps you have always held a special place in your heart for me." She felt him waver just slightly. "We should sit down."

He shook his head. "Not yet." He bent his head to kiss her gently. "I rather like the feeling of holding you like this."

"Mmmm. I like it, too, but your leg will grow weary as mine are doing. I find I would like a rest." She helped him to a bench along the wall of the house. "I have also evaluated my own actions."

"You have?"

She nodded.

"And what have you found?"

She clasped his hand between hers. "It is silly, really." She gave a small, embarrassed laugh. "When I would play with my dolls, their father's name was always Richard.and Darcy was always their uncle." She glanced at him and saw his amused smile. "I told you it was silly."

He shook his head. "It is not silly," he assured her though he did laugh softly. "So tell me, was this Richard a good father?"

She bit her lip and ducked her head slightly. "Not always. The mother had to scold the father sometimes for allowing the children to do things that ruined their clothes. He even let them eat sweets before supper and skip lessons to play games. Can you imagine?" She looked up at him, her eyes sparkling with amusement.

His whole body shook as he laughed, and she joined him. "I can."

"I think it is because I always longed to do those things." She leaned into his shoulder.

"And I would have let you while Darcy would have preached duty."

She nodded. "I believe you would have." She sat silently for a moment, contemplating the man next to her as a father. "You will make a fine father," she said at last. "Darcy will, too, and with Elizabeth as a mother, his children may have a hope of having as much fun as ours."

He lifted her hand to his lips. "And you will scold me when I allow them too much fun?"

"Of course. I am my mother's daughter and very good at scolding."

He chuckled. "Yes, I have endured your scolding before." He looked to see who had come to join them on the terrace. "And I have also endured Darcy's." He leaned toward her and kissed her, long and deeply and slowly, completely ignoring the throat clearing sounds Darcy was making.

~*~*~*~*~*~

Mrs. Jenkins fastened the string of pearls behind Anne's neck. "You look lovely," she said as she looked at her former charge in the glass. "I had always hoped to see you as a happy bride."

Anne turned and clasped the hands of her friend. "And now you have, for I am a very happy bride. I pray you will have as much success with your new charge."

Mrs. Jenkins sighed. "Miss Barrows is exuberant and does not lack the ability to put herself forward, but she lacks refinement."

Anne laughed. "She will do well with you to guide her. When does her brother arrive?"

"We are expected to meet him in London by week's end. He is much like his father, so I expect we shall get on quite well."

"And how does she accept the absence of her mother and father?"

"There are tears, but they are not so frequent as they once were."

Anne patted Mrs. Jenkins' hand. "You were always very good at comforting me, and you were often more a mother to me than my own was. Miss Barrows is fortunate."

There was a soft rap at the door to the sitting room.

"Mr. Darcy." Mrs. Jenkins dipped her head slightly in greeting as she opened the door. She smiled at Anne and slipped out.

"Are you ready?" Darcy pulled out his pocket watch and looked at the time.

Anne raised an eyebrow and folded her arms across her chest. The tapping of her toe drew his attention away from his timepiece.

He crossed the room to her. "Aside from the scowl, you look lovely, Cousin." He kissed her cheek.

"Thank you." She walked to the window that overlooked the garden. "We have time. You are not late unless you arrive after the bride."

He chuckled and took a seat. "Has your mother heard of this theory?"

Anne looked over her shoulder at him. "She has; though, she does not approve."

"I thought as much."

"She will no doubt be along to fetch me if I do not appear when she thinks I should." She turned and leaned against the window frame. "It was not long ago that we met here just like this."

"And you were waiting for your mother then as well." He stretched out his legs in front of him and crossed them at the ankles.

"And you were rather more anxious that day." She came to take the seat next to him.

"As were you."

"Indeed." She laughed. "I shall never forget the shock I gave you when I told you Mr. Collins had been married. I thought I had gone too far in my attempts to discover your feelings for Elizabeth."

He grimaced. "I admit I had trouble breathing and thought my heart might just cease its beating."

"I am sorry." She laid her hand on his arm.

"I am not." He covered her hand with his. "For in that moment, I knew my heart would not survive without her."

She smiled at him. "We have both found our heart's desire, have we not?"

"Indeed we have."

She rose as she heard the clickity clack of her mother's shoes in the hall. "It will be your day soon," she said to him as she smoothed her skirt.

He beamed at her and extended his arm. "Just three more weeks."

"And Bingley will join you?"

"That is the reason for the delay. Elizabeth and Jane wished to share their day with a double ceremony."

"And you cannot deny her a thing," Anne teased.

"I tried." His face took on a bit of a rosy hue. "I was not pleased with the delay."

She laughed.

"Anne…" Her mother's reprimand about minding her time died on her lips as she opened the door. She dabbed at her eyes with her handkerchief. "Oh, you are so beautiful!" She clasped her handkerchief to her heart. Excitement shone in her eyes. "Imagine, your wedding day has finally arrived!" She cast a stern glance at Darcy. "No thanks to you, Darcy." She winked at Anne as Darcy rolled his eyes.

"Mama, it was not his doing. He is not the one who..."

Lady Catherine clucked her tongue. "It is not fitting to speak of unpleasant memories on a day such as this." She gave them both a nudge toward the door. "Today is as it should be. There is no better day than the day you marry the one for whom your heart yearns." She sighed.

Anne shook her head in wonder. She still had not gotten used to the changes in her mother. She would miss her when she moved away. She and Mr. Cranfield had married only two days ago and would be leaving on the morrow. They would begin their life together near where his boats docked before travelling on to London at the end of summer.

She smiled and felt a laugh bubble up inside her as she and Darcy began descending the stairs. She was recalling the reaction of both Darcy and Elizabeth to the news that Mr. Cranfield owned a very nice home near Cheapside, not too far from where Elizabeth's Aunt and Uncle Gardiner lived. This fact combined with the comment Lady Catherine had made about hosting her new niece, Miss Bingley, and assisting her in her search for a husband was more that the two could countenance without dissolving into an extended bout of laughter. Richard did his best to explain the reason for their laughter while Lady Catherine shook her head and declared that Miss Bingley's attitude was not to be borne — which again caused general laughter among those who knew Miss Bingley.

Her stomach did a little flip as she reached the bottom of the stairs, and they faced the door to the drawing room where Mr. Collins and Richard, as well as a few assembled guests, awaited her.

"Are you well?" asked Darcy noticing her pause.

She nodded, a smile suffusing her face. "I have never been better." She waited while her mother slipped into the room and took her place next to Mr. Cranfield. Then it was time for her to join Richard in front of the garden doors where he stood propped on his crutches with Mr. Collins. She pulled back slightly on Darcy's arm. He looked at her, his brows furrowed.

"Thank you."

"For what?"

"For helping me find my own happiness."

"You're welcome, but I did very little to assist you." He looked at her face and then Richard's. "Happiness often follows when you listen."

"Listen?" She looked up at him in confusion. "To what?"

He smiled at her and tipped his head toward Richard. "To your heart," he said as he began leading her into the room. "Always, listen to your heart."

Acknowledgements

Thank you to the many people who have shared in the creation of this work.

To individually thank all the readers and friends who have encouraged me on this journey would be nearly impossible. However, I would be remiss if I did not mention a few. First, there is my invaluable team of beta's, Kathryn, Betty, and Rose. These ladies checked facts, story elements, punctuation, spelling and grammar before handing it back over to me to adjust and refine and edit again. Next, there is my online writing buddy and cheerleader, Zoe, who often talked me away from the delete key and checked wording on random sentences. Then, there are my readers from forums and my blog, who faithfully read and commented on the story as I posted it piece by piece. It was such an encouragement to hear their thoughts and ideas. Finally, and most importantly, I must thank my husband for his loving and somewhat pushy support of my writing–without his insistence that I share my work, this book may not have come to be.

About the Author

Leenie Brown has always been a girl with an active imagination, which, while growing up, was a both an asset, providing many hours of fun as she played out stories, and a liability, when her older sister and aunt would tell her frightening tales. At one time, they had her convinced Dracula lived in the trunk at the end of the bed she slept in when visiting her grandparents!

Although it has been years since she cowered in her bed in her grandparents' basement, she still has an imagination which occasionally runs away with her, and she feeds it now as she did then — by reading!

Her heroes, when growing up, were authors, and the worlds they painted with words were (and still are) her favourite playgrounds! She was that child, under the covers with the flashlight, reading until the wee hours of the morning…and pretending not to be tired the next day so her mother wouldn't find out. Today, she fits, or is that squeezes, reading in around caring for her family of two fabulous (most of the time) teenage boys and one sweet and thoughtful husband while working as a junior-high teacher .

In addition to feeding her imagination, she also exercises it —by writing. While writing has been an activity she has dabbled in over the years, it blossomed into a full-fledged obsession when she stumbled upon the world of Jane Austen Fan Fiction. As the second born of five sisters, just like Elizabeth Bennet, her imagination was soon captured. And now, she spends much time in the regency world, playing with the characters from her favourite Jane Austen novels and a few that are of her own creation.

When she is not traipsing down a trail in an attempt to keep up with her imagination, she resides in the beautiful province of Nova Scotia .

Connect with Leenie Brown

E-mail:
LeenieBrownAuthor@gmail.com

Twitter:
@LeenieBAuthor

Facebook:
www.facebook.com/LeenieBrownAuthor

Blog:
leeniebrown.com

More from Leenie Brown

OXFORD COTTAGE

Elizabeth Bennet expects to complete the challenge her father has set before her at Oxford Cottage. What she does not expect is to meet a handsome stranger and fall in love, nor does she expect to find herself in a situation where she will have to keep both herself and her young companion safe.

FOR PEACE OF MIND

After refusing Mr. Collins' offer of marriage, Elizabeth Bennet is sent to stay with her aunt and uncle in London. While there, she finds both love and opposition. Can she keep both her love and her peace of mind?

TEATIME TALES

A collection of six short and sweet Austen-inspired stories intended to be a light pick-me-up.

THROUGH EVERY STORM

Coming September 2015

Wickham is a changed man, but his wife has yet to leave some of her childish ways behind. Can a former wastrel redeem both himself and his wife?

Made in the USA
Middletown, DE
24 November 2015